This Secret Between Us

Harper Rae James

Cover design: Harper Rae James

First edition 2025

Printed in the United States of America

ISBN: 979-8-9918148-4-3

Playlist

FOR AN IMMERSIVE READING experience, please enjoy this playlist on Spotify.

Happy Reading,
Harper

Trigger Warnings

D EAR READER,

Before you begin, I want to offer a gentle heads-up about some of the themes explored in this story. This book contains emotional and intimate content that may be difficult for some readers, including:

- Infertility and the emotional impact surrounding it

- Characters grappling with inexperience and vulnerability around intimacy

- Public play (sexual content in semi-public settings)

- A scene where a sex dream transitions into real sexual activity while both characters are in a sleep-heavy or semi-conscious state

These elements are handled with care, but I recognize they may not be for everyone. Please take care of yourself and read at your own comfort level.

With love,
Harper

Dedication

This one's for every woman who builds walls up to keep her heart safe. You deserve the world! Break those motherfuckers down and dance in the rubble!

Prologue

July, Six Months Ago...

Cash

"**W**HAT HAPPENED WITH THE redhead you left with last night?" Austin asks with a suggestive wiggle of his brow.

"Don't worry about it," I suggest clearly closing the door on that conversation. I don't broadcast my sex life. "Oh, now that I have my phone, look at the video I was telling you about last night. The one of me in the cage with my Torpedo," I said, changing the subject.

"Fuck yeah. How is she? Amazing?" He takes the bait and forgets all about trying to get the details of my hook up with Blake.

"Yeah, she's great, but fuck, something just feels off. Maybe I rushed into it. I thought she was the right fit but now I'm wondering if I just got caught up in the moment."

"You seemed into it last night." He chuckles. He's such a sucker for a new bat.

"I was," I let out a deep sigh, "I mean, don't get me wrong, she's got a great feel. She looks good, but that only gets you so far. She was just kind of under-whelming, ya know? I don't want to waste my time on something that's not worth it. Is she really 'game day' material?"

"Yeah, plus you're not really the kind of guy to stick with only one…" His words trail off as he starts watching the video.

"True. What if she's not worth the hype?" I genuinely asked.

I lean over the table so I can watch the video with him as Blake walks past our table, flips me off and heads out the door.

"I take it last night didn't go well." Austin laughs as he briefly glances up from the video on my phone.

What the fuck was that about?

I contemplate going after her. Seeing what changed since last night, but is that what you do in this situation? I've never had a one-night stand, maybe she's upset I left. Was I supposed to stay? Do you cuddle after a hookup?

Fuck.

I run my fingers through my hair not knowing what the right move is.

"You gonna text her?" Austin asks.

"I don't have her number." I pause thinking about my limited options at the moment. "Should I have gone after her? Is it too late now?" I ask.

"She's probably gone," he adds. "Shit man, that crushes the ball." He clearly could give two shits about this predicament I'm in.

I turn and look out the window, but there is no sign of her outside. I try to convince myself that if I lived here, I'd have gone after her, but in all reality I wouldn't have known what to say. So I fall back against the back of the booth and stay put.

Maybe it's for the best.

November

Two Months Ago...

Cash

T HERE IS NO BETTER feeling than beating the shit out of a punching bag after a long day.

Correction, there is only one thing better, but I don't have any current prospects for that at the moment, so a boxing class wins.

"Shit, where the hell is my wallet?" I wonder as I look all over my Airbnb. When I went to dinner with Knox, I had it. I just paid.

> **Cash:** Any chance my wallet fell out in your car?

I continue looking while I wait for Knox's response, tracing every single step I took when I got home.

It's not in my work bag.

Not on the nightstand.

Not on the bathroom counter.

I was pretty distracted when I made my protein shake. Maybe I left it in the fridge.

Ding.

I walk over to my phone and read the text from Knox.

> **Knox:** Yup. Just found it wedged between the seat and console.

> **Cash:** Okay. I'll come by and get it before you leave.

> **Knox:** Too late. We got here a few minutes ago. Just text me when you get here, and I'll bring it out to you.

> **Cash:** Sounds good. Be there in a few.

I grab my shake off the counter and head out to my car.

Knox, one of my best friends from college, and his wife Ana, are going to the opening of Blake's bookstore tonight. It should be a great night. A small part of me wishes I was invited, but that's not happening.

Hooking up with her is something I wish I had gotten to do more than once. She was stunning the night of Knox and Ana's wedding. The night was electric; the kind fueled by whiskey and our bodies pressed close all night on the dance floor. Too bad shit went sideways. I just wish I knew why.

Blake was a breath of fresh air in a cloud of self-tanner, face powder, and perfume that most women bathe in to get the attention of professional athletes. She doesn't give a fuck what anyone thinks and is unapologetically herself.

She enjoys sex, and I enjoyed the hell out of it with her. She was irresistible. Too bad I lost my chance. Now, a few months later, she's dating Luke, and from what I can tell, they're made for each other.

Tonight she's opening Lit and Libations, and I'm so damn happy for her. According to Ana, when they were roommates, she had an entire closet in their apartment stocked with things for the bar she would open one day, and Knox has told me how much work she has put into this, and I think it's amazing. I'm also pretty sure I am the last person she wants to see tonight, given our past encounters, so I have to be in and out.

I pull up in front of Lit and Libations and send Knox a text.

Cash: Here

The building is exactly what I would expect from Blake, encompassing her flair and charm. The worn and weathered red brick building is picturesque, with black metal framing the picture windows. There are flower pots out front that enhance the elegance, draping over the pots in bright, vibrant colors.

Wondering what is taking Knox so long, I look at the clock in my car.

Shit. My boxing class starts in 20 minutes.

I pick up the phone and call him, but he doesn't answer.

The number one stipulation in my contract that allowed me to work with this foundation was that I would work out every day, so I would be in prime shape for games when I travel back home. The Sun Cats' manager is no joke, and he ensured he was a secondary member on my membership so he could keep tabs on my regimen. If I miss tonight, I can guarantee a phone call from him bright and early tomorrow morning, wondering what the fuck I was up to and questioning if working with the foundation is in my best interest.

For me, working with the foundation is personal, something I can do to honor Knox after he lost his chance to play. Watching my best friend struggle with his baseball career being cut short is something I'll never forget. With him opening a new youth training facility, having this program here is essential to me.

The Empowering Versatile Athletes foundation is one of a kind. Their mission—right there in the name. The EVA's main objective is to create a rehab center in local hospitals across the country where athletes of all levels can have access to post-injury rehabilitation, mental health and overall wellness care. They reached out to the MLB seeking partnership, and to me the opportunity was a simple decision. I volunteered immediately.

I sit for a few more minutes waiting for a response, and after several minutes, nothing.

I would do almost anything for Knox, but waiting here and jeopardising my ability to work with the foundation is not one of them.

Against my better judgment, I decide to head inside, find Knox, and get lost as fast as possible.

I exit the car and walk up to the entrance, head down trying not to be noticed.

"Shit, sorry," I say as I bump into a small figure right in front of the building, and when I look up, I meet eyes with the most beautiful blonde I have ever seen.

Time feels like it stops. I can hear the beat of my heart thrumming in my ears, and all I want is to stand here and find out more about who she is.

Holy Shit! She is—

"What the fuck are you doing here?" Her abrupt tone interrupts my thoughts.

Wait. Do I know her? I'm positive I've never seen her before. Her plump pink lips and curly blonde hair dusting her shoulders are a sight I would never forget. I'm sure of it.

Not knowing what to say, I put my hand out to shake hers. "Hi, I'm—"

She instantly cuts me off and moves past me. "I know who you are, you piece of shit. You're Cash, the douchebag that screwed with Blake's head. *Why* are you here?" she repeats.

What? Shit. She's feisty, and I think I like it.

"I just came to get my wallet from Knox." I lean around her and open the door.

She is reluctant to walk in, probably to be seen with me, so I let her go first, but when she trips on uneven ground just before she walks through the door, I place my hand on the small of her back to steady her. Despite her angry words, she seems almost thankful for my touch.

Knox is standing at the bar, not too far from the door, so I make my way over to him, and Ana looks up and beckons to this gorgeous blonde, simultaneously calling her over.

"April," Ana waves.

Her name is just as fucking stunning as she is. She looks like April. Bright blonde hair, kissed by the sun, full pink lips, and from what I can tell from her, the way she greeted Ana, a bubbly personality. A stark contrast to the disdain I got from her a few moments ago.

"Sorry, man. I just saw your calls and texts," Knox says, breaking my trance as he hands me my wallet. Just as I turn to leave, Ana speaks over the music.

"Oh, my God. Are you two here together?" Her voice is loud and booming just as the music pauses before the crescendo.

I feel all eyes move in our direction, and before either of us can answer, I am struck in the fucking face by a fist. My vision blurs and the room spins at warp speed.

"What the fuck was that for?" I yell, holding my chin, only to look up and see Luke standing there with anger lacing his expression. Luke is not only Blake's new boyfriend, he is also supervising my volunteer work at the hospital, and getting into a fight with him will not look good for me, as a professional athlete, in my work with the foundation, or the hospital for that matter.

Fuck.

I step back away from Luke and take a deep breath, rubbing the place on my jaw that is going to bruise. I can feel it. I try to regain my composure instead of hitting him back in the fucking face like I want to. Too much is at stake.

Luckily, Knox steps in between me and Luke, confusion etched across his face. With his other hand, he nudges Ana back and looks at April.

"Get her the fuck away from here," he demands, gesturing for April to move Ana away from the fight. She's pregnant with their second baby and has no business being caught up in this shitshow.

"How fucking dare you, you fucking piece of shit!" Luke yells, reaching for me. "You fucking belittled her, made her feel like she was not fucking worthy of love, shattering the most precious thing in the world."

I can't keep up. Who? Blake? How did I shatter her?

"You had pure fucking perfection in your hands and you fucking treated it like trash. And now you have the fucking audacity to show up here with my little sister! She is not a fucking toy to play with Cash, your next fucking conquest."

Luke reaches out and punches me again, only this time he has to reach around Knox's head. Somehow, I'm not sure how he managed, the punch lands a little harder and draws blood from my lip.

"What the hell are you talking about?" I give him a slanted look, now pissed, and so fucking confused.

The blonde is his sister? What the hell did I just walk into?

Wiping the blood with my hand, I stand stunned and motionless.

What the fuck did I miss?

My pulse quickens, and I am suddenly hyper-aware of my pulse thrumming in my chest, neck, hell, I can even feel it in my fingertips.

I look around and survey the stares in the room full of strangers, and they feel cold and unwelcoming. Usually I welcome the gaze of strangers; it feels good to be noticed as a professional athlete. They make me feel like somebody. But right now, they're looking at me like the scum on the bottom of their shoe.

Fuck, if any of them recognize me, this is going to be a nightmare. I duck my head in an attempt to hide my face.

How the hell did I become the villain here?

"Knock it the fuck off. Both of you!" Knox yells. He grabs me by the shirt and pushes me towards the door. "What the fuck is he talking about, Cash?" The look on Knox's face is pure fucking murder.

I look at Knox, blood on my lip. Fists clenched at my side. And for the first time in a long time, I realize something: I don't know shit about the damage I've done.

Do You Even Hear Me?

January 3rd

"Yeah we got friendship, the kind that last a lifetime."
-Chris Stapleton

April

"Hi Mom." I lean in and give my mom the biggest hug when I walk into their house for dinner. My mom has always been my safe place to land, and tonight, I think I'm going to need her more than ever. We have family dinner every Sunday, but this is the first one Blake and I will be at together in a while. We made up, but things are still a little off between us and I can't quite figure out why. My mom is a great buffer, and loves us both unconditionally, so she will make sure everything is smooth tonight.

Blake and I laugh, we joke, we talk about things that seemingly don't matter to anyone else in the room, but family dinners are just the five of us. It's intimate, and the layers of frayed edges in our friendship unravel a little more the more time that passes, and lately I'm at a loss for what exactly the root of it is. We cleared the air about her and Luke's relationship, but something else is lingering.

Mom wraps me in her arms, and I get lost in the familiar smell of her Chanel No.5 perfume, instant comfort.

"Where is Cash, baby girl? At some point, you need to bring him around so we can get to know him better. It's time we all get past this mess." Her voice is soft and velvety, and it usually brings me so much peace, but right now it's sparking confusion.

What? They think we're dating?

The sound of his name makes my blood run cold. Not a soul has mentioned him in two months. I guess I just assumed they all knew better and realized it was a misunderstanding. Things were tense after that night, and Blake and I were already in uncharted territory with her dating my brother, so that means I handled it the best way I know how, avoided it entirely.

This, I didn't see coming.

Not long after Blake's grand opening, my brother proposed, and when the attention shifted to planning their upcoming nuptials and no one else brought it up, I didn't either. Oops! Guess I should have clarified I was not there with him.

Mom clears her throat, waiting for my response, and it shoots me right back into the present.

"Mom, we're not dating. It was all a terrible misunderstanding."

"*Sure*," she coos with a wiggle of her brow as if she doesn't believe a word coming out of my mouth, "but I know you, sweetie, and you hate conflict. Things got a little out of control and escalated quickly at the opening.

I told everyone just to let it be and not to bring it up so you could have time to process it all." She places her hands on both sides of my face. "April, look at me. You deserve to be happy, regardless of the circumstances." She gives me a hug. "Besides, your brother said he overheard Cash talking about you at the hospital. Apparently, he thinks you are impossibly beautiful. Sweetie, enough time has gone by that we can all take a breath and be mature adults."

Cash is a baseball player, a freaking professional athlete. He could have anyone in the world. Not to mention one tiny little detail, we haven't seen each other since the opening. My mom might be dreaming, because let's be real, after 2 months, he probably doesn't even remember me. I bet his comment my brother overheard was the next day.

With that little anecdote, she turns and heads to the living room where Dad, Luke, and Blake are visiting.

"You deserve to be happy regardless of the circumstances." Her words gut me, and she doesn't even know it. She thinks she uncovered my life story, but is missing the plot twist.

When I walk in, I catch my brother brushing her hair from her face so he can get a better look at her, and my heart melts for them. I wish everyone had a love like theirs, especially me, but that's not my current reality, contrary to the apparent belief of my family.

BEEP. BEEP.

The shrill high-pitched sound of my alarm breaks the silence.

I quickly clear my screen before anyone sees the text that feels like it can be seen from 10 miles away.

Note to self, escape to the bathroom later to order my prescription refill.

Clearing my mind of my actual reality, I ponder why Cash didn't set the record straight with my brother, and then I realize, given how mad my brother was that night, Cash was probably not in a hurry to risk having a conversation at the hospital.

"There's my little ray of sunshine," Dad smiles as he rises from his chair to give me a hug.

My dad is a powerful man with a large frame, and when he wraps his arms around me, I feel like a little kid again, something that I really need at the moment as I try to figure out how to clear up this little mess.

As soon as he releases me, my brother is quick to steal me away. "Ap, come see this. You're never going to believe it." He pulls me through the house and out to the back deck, leaving Blake and my parents to visit. Thankful for the momentary reprieve, I follow him to the backyard.

"What?" I gawk, peering through the flurry of snow drifting softly from the sky. "A hot tub? When did they get a hot tub? I was here two days ago, and they didn't even mention they bought one," I say with surprise as I walk out the back door.

"Right? All we wanted growing up was a hot tub, and they always had a million excuses for not wanting to get one," Luke laughs.

Despite our age difference, Luke and I have always been close. He is more than a big brother to me. He's one of my best friends. The only other best friend I have is the redhead he is marrying, sitting inside with my parents. Blake had a rough childhood and spent most days here with my family. She's probably inside joking with them about the hot tub right now.

Luke knows me better than most, so he notices that something's wrong, only he doesn't exactly know why.

"It's going to be okay, you know," he says with a smile.

"What?" I ask.

"You and Blake."

"We made up; we're fine, Luke."

"No, you're not, and you both know it. You made up, but you're still keeping each other at arm's length, even with your new relationship with Cash."

Mom appears in the doorway, almost as if she meant to interrupt our conversation, creating an awkward silence.

"It's time to eat." She smiles, and Luke immediately turns towards the door. Even at almost 40, he has the appetite of a teenager.

For fuck's sake.

Frustrated, I huff and make my way inside. I know I should have addressed this two months ago, but two months goes by fast. Now it feels too late.

We eat and visit and laugh through dinner, as if nothing changed. Except for the fact that Blake is sitting on the other side of the table next to Luke instead of next to me, where she usually sits.

Mom made cookies, and there is a lull in the conversation as everyone tries to find room to indulge in the sweet treat. The smell of warm cookies is my absolute favorite. It's calming and inviting, and right now that's the vibe I'm chasing.

Suddenly Blake speaks up, breaking the silence, and the words that come out of her mouth stun me. "So, how is Cash?"

I choke on my cookie. I finish chewing so I can respond; she takes it as an opportunity to continue.

"Listen, I know it's hard to admit when you fall for someone and think your best friend won't understand," she smiles at my brother. "April, you and I have been here before, and if he is good to you, that's all that matters."

I immediately interject, "Bullshit. That is not all that matters."

Blake takes a deep breath and closes her eyes as if she is trying to find strength deep down that she isn't sure she has. "April, I'm trying here. I expect to see him at the wedding, okay? I really want you to be happy." Her smile is soft and full of love. It's a glimpse of the best friend I have been missing, the one that will put all of her baggage aside to be in my corner. I just wish they would all stop making fucking assumptions and let me speak.

"Blake, he is not—"

"It's okay," she interrupts.

Why, why do I even try to explain this to any of them? Fuck it.

I sigh, not wanting to fight this battle anymore. "You know what, okay? He will be there. I'm done talking about this." I sigh with a half-hearted smile. "Daddy, tell me about this hot tub in the backyard."

What the hell was I just thinking? He won't be there. Fuck.

But the conversation quickly shifts, not leaving room for me to correct myself, and as they all laugh at something Dad said, I realize I didn't hear any of it.

Cash

FUCK, I'M SO TIRED. I wonder whether the pizza I ordered last week is still good. I don't feel like putting any effort into dinner right now.

My phone vibrates in my pocket, and when I look down, Anderson's face pops up on the screen. Anderson, always the PR manager, is probably calling to make sure I'm upholding a flawless reputation during my stay here in Vermont.

But every time he calls, my stomach lurches. It's been quite a while since the fight at Blake's opening, and he's yet to mention it. Which means no one at the bar that night leaked video. They all appeared to be close friends and family of Blake, so I'm not too worried, but fuck me if I don't panic a little each time he calls to check in. If he catches wind of that fight, he'll put a stop to this entire thing, sending me home.

"What's up, man?" I greet him with a cheery tone, setting my exhaustion to the side for a moment.

"Just checking in. Any new updates?" he inquires.

"Nope, just starting my rotation on the pediatric floor in about two weeks."

"Great! We've heard nothing but good things from your supervisor."

I breathe a sigh of relief. Luke could easily give me a critical review, and I'd be out of here.

The walk from my car to my apartment door feels like rounding third in a heatwave doubleheader, and I'm trying not to let my calm and collected mask slip. A task that is only made harder by the dropping temperatures outside.

"Awesome. I have—" I'm so damn tired, I'm even seeing things. That looks like April pacing outside the doors to my apartment building… Wait, it is her. She must be freezing. She spins around and the second she gets a glimpse of me, she doesn't even wait for me to get closer before darting in my direction. That beautiful mouth of hers just starts talking a million miles a minute, and my tired brain has a hard time keeping up.

"Oh, thank God. I thought I was going to be here for hours waiting for you," her voice bellows. "It's cold as shit out here."

"Listen, Anderson, I have to go. I have to see if this lady needs help. Thanks for calling." I don't wait for his response. I hang up in a panic as April approaches.

"How do you know where I'm staying?" I ask her as I look around, slightly concerned that she could track me down this easily.

"Knox mentioned how beautiful the Cedar Crest apartments were that you were staying in, so I looked them up. I didn't know which one was yours, so…"

"Are you a cleat chaser?" My heart pumps out of my chest, a nervous feeling taking over. I've never had someone show up like this, but a few of my teammates have, and the idea always terrified me.

"What?" She shakes her head. "No. God no, Cash. Chasing you down has nothing to do with me wanting to get in your bed." She scrunches her nose in disgust. "Are you that full of yourself? I need your help."

Shit, she talks fast.

"Okay, first off, I need you to take a damn breath. I'm exhausted, and I can't process this fast." I watch her. She closes her eyes and follows my request. Her long eyelashes dance against her face with each breath. The same bubble gum pink that caught my attention two months ago paints her lips today. I vividly remember the way it drew me in. The fullness of her lips was stunning in the dark with only the street lights illuminating them, but this time, she tied her honey hair in a sleek ponytail, so nothing is blocking my view. Damn, she's pretty.

"What is going on?" I ask, snapping myself out of my own thoughts before I'm too far gone.

"I need you to do me a favor, and you can't say no." She almost looks like she is going to cry.

"Ok."

"Cash, pleas— Wait, what?" She looks at me shocked.

"Well, you fucking hate me, so if you're here, you are obviously desperate, and it's not like you are going to ask me to be your boyfriend or some crazy shit like that."

She just stares back at me with a devious look on her face.

I'm not sure what she is plotting, but man, do I want to.

"What?" I ask, now feeling a little unsteady.

"Well, I do *fucking* hate you, but everyone believes we are dating—"

"No," I interrupt.

"You didn't even let me finish," she scoffs.

"Let's go inside where we can sit down and talk, and you can warm up," I suggest, walking to my apartment as she follows right behind.

"Look, I was lucky to escape disaster after your brother punched me. I'm not tempting fate." Unlocking the door, my words trail off when I look at her and see the fury building in her eyes.

"You already said you would do it. You really are a piece of shit," she scoffs. "You treat Blake like shit, show up at her opening knowing you're not wanted there, and cause a scene—"

"I caused a scene? I was picking up my wallet from Knox, and got sucker punched."

"Well, now they all think we are dating, and every time—" She pauses, visibly fighting back tears, and her eyes well up making my heart ache.

"Cash, I'm in over my head and *need* your help," she says the words with such desperation I break.

"Help, how?" I ask with a sigh. I pinch the bridge of my nose as she begins to speak, and her words leave me speechless.

"Come to the wedding in Jamaica with me, as my *boyfriend*," she winces.

"Are you serious? Are you trying to cause a fight at your brother's wedding?"

"It was Blake's idea, she insisted," her voice starts to pick up pace again, "she said you can't hide forever, and she expects to see you at the wedding."

"This sounds like a terrible idea." I run my hands over my face, trying to make sense of this whole thing.

"Yes, it does, but having to endure half conversations for a week where they fill in what they believe as truths sounds worse," her voice is shaky. "I think they're so fucking excited that I've *settled down,*" she uses air quotes to punctuate her words, "that they actually don't give a shit who it's with. Plus, I already said you were coming."

She looks at me with those bright blue eyes, and I can't help the words that tumble out of my mouth. "Fine, but

I don't want to give everyone another reason to hate me, so we have to make it believable."

"They already believe it, so all we have to do is show up." Her words are so perky and sure.

Well, that was quite the mood shift.

"You don't think we should, oh I don't know, get to know each other and look like an actual couple?" I ask, sarcasm clear in my voice.

"No. I already have to pretend I like you in public. I have absolutely no interest in pretending when we're alone."

"April, they are going to expect us to know a bit about each other, have stories to share, and shit like that."

"They will probably continue to fill in the blanks themselves. That's why we're in this mess. I doubt they'll want to hear what I have to say now." Frustration fills her expression.

"April—" She cuts me off with a wave of her hand.

She starts to walk away, and it irritates the shit out of me.

"Not listening must be a family trait," I whisper under my breath as my eyes roll back in my head.

As if she heard me, she stops and her words come perfectly on cue. "If they ask us questions, we will divert attention back to Blake and Luke. I mean, they are the ones getting married. The attention should be on them, anyway. We will stage a fight on the way home and break up. Easy peasy."

Without another word, she turns and continues to walk away. She makes it about another ten steps before she turns around for the second time. "I'll text you all the details. We leave in four days."

What the fuck?

"You don't have my number," I yell after her.

"I'll get it from Knox."

This can't possibly end well. But maybe that's the point.

I Really Do Hate You!

"The trouble with girls is they're a mystery
Something about them puzzles me"

-Scotty McCreery

April

Ugh… I know Cash is right. We need to get to know each other if we want to pull this off. I also know this is fucking insane, but I need to save face. It's gotten to the point where this feels like the only logical way out. I've never been good at facing difficult situations. It's a real problem. It's why Ana and Knox broke up, and why Blake and I are barely talking. I can't seem to clear up misunderstandings or share important details to save my life.

That thought and my increased anxiety sets in. Before Knox met Ana, he and I offered a great distraction from life for one another, just when I needed it most. The best part, it was casual. Casual is all I will allow myself. But it all came crashing down when my inability to clear the air when confrontation arose and I made a mess of things.

And just like that, I'm spiraling into the past. Back to the night I blew up Knox and Ana's relationship before they even had a shot.

"Oh, anxiety," I think to myself, because nothing says fun like overthinking shit from the past.

"Knox," I yell above the music.

"Hey, April. What are you doing here? I didn't know you and Ethan knew each other?"

"Who's Ethan?"

"My roommate, this is his parents' party. They moved in here a few years ago."

"Weird! We've never met, but I love his mom! I thought you lived at home?" I ask, but I'm too drunk to focus on his response. "Anyway, there is someone…"

Suddenly, his attention shifts without warning, and he darts across the room with an urgency I had never seen. "Excuse me," he says, moving past me.

I watch him approach Blake and her friend Ana.

I wonder how he knows them.

Not thinking too much of it, I join them. I was planning on introducing them, anyway.

"Knox, this is who I wanted you to meet," I say, pointing to Blake. "Blake and I have been friends since our sopho-more year in high school. She moved about 45 minutes from here after college, so we don't see each other very often anymore." Just then, I notice his hand is intertwined with Blake's friend Ana's. "How do you two know each other?"

Well, this is awkward, *I think to myself.*

Ana doesn't hesitate in her response. "Knox and I met at the bar I work at a few weeks ago, and we've been hanging out since."

"Oh well," I say, "the way he's holding your hand, I thought it might be more serious, and that would be really awkward." I sigh.

Ana gives me a curious look as Knox drags her away.

I spend the next several hours drinking and playing beer pong in the garage when, suddenly, Knox catches my eye.

Damn, he looks so good.

I walk towards him, deciding to shoot my shot at not going home alone tonight. Being alone sends my mind to places I'd rather ignore.

He's alone, so Ana must have lost interest.

When he heads to the bathroom, I decide to follow, excited for a little more privacy.

"Knox," I say, pushing my way into the bathroom behind him. I know I'm drunk, but he doesn't waste any time, and I'm here for it. He's already undone his pants and has his cock out as the door clicks shut.

Sometimes it's hard for me to get in the mood, but I get turned on after a few drinks. My panties dampen at the sight of him.

"What the fuck, April, get out of here," he says with a laugh. Knox playing hard to get wasn't on my bingo card for us tonight, but it could be fun.

"What?" I tease, pulling my top down.

"April…" his words trail off and mush together in my mind. I'm too focused on the thought of his cock to truly focus on any of the words coming out of his mouth. He's probably just worried that I'm too drunk.

"Well, since you have it out," I say, trying to reach over and grab his dick, to prove I know what I'm doing. I may not have experienced an orgasm myself, but I love giving them.

"April!" he shouts with a little chuckle, the change in his tone catches my attention, "Listen, Ana and I are not official, but I really like her, so this," he says, pointing between us, "this is done."

Suddenly I realize he's shoving his dick back in his pants and fastening them as he opens the door, leaving me, tits out, trying to register what he said.

Shit, he actually likes her.

If I were sober, I probably would have picked up on it better. I look like such a bitch right now.

"Knox, wai—" but Ana's stunned face interrupts my attempt to smooth things over with him. Hurt fills her eyes as she locks them with mine. She immediately turns and walks towards the door.

No, no, no. Shit.

I stand frozen, unable to process what just unfolded in front of me.

It took longer than it should have for me to go to Blake and Ana's apartment to clear the air, but by that point, Ana and Knox had already broken up.

"Why are you such a coward?" I ask myself, disappointed I can't seem to keep myself out of unnecessary drama. I know that nothing good will come of pretending that Cash and I are dating, but trying to convince myself of that is no use. It's already in motion, right?

Deciding against asking Knox for Cash's phone number, I drive back over to Cash's apartment. I don't want to involve Knox. He would immediately know we're not dating and could never lie to Ana. As shitty as it is that I'm lying to everyone, it would be even shittier to bring Knox and Ana into and expect them to lie for me.

Here's to letting the lies roll.

My hands are shaky, and my heart is racing as I walk up to the door. I almost turned around three times, talking myself out of it. It would have probably been the smarter choice, but common sense is something I am severely lacking.

To my surprise, he's home and answers the door seconds after I knock.

"Hey, what are you doing here?" he says with obvious confusion across his face. "Did you realize this is a bad idea and change your mind?"

He wishes. To be honest, I do too.

"Shut up," I say, pushing my way inside. I can't believe I am doing this. He is such a tool.

I take in his apartment, last time I was here, I was far too flustered to notice the details. It looks less like a place someone lives, and more like an Airbnb waiting for its next guest. The lighting catches the bare white walls, making the space cold and uninviting. The furniture is simple with sharp corners, giving off a minimalist vibe, but not in a cool way.

Who picks this as a place to stay, literally out of a virtual catalog of places?

I shake my head, an effort to refocus, my brain fog is getting a little out of control. "You were right. We need a story, so we have three days to date. Where are you taking me first?"

Cash

W HY IS SHE SUCH a fucking pain in the ass?

"You just assume I am free to be at your beck and call?" I scoff, slightly annoyed by her assessment.

"Do you have plans?" she asks sarcastically as she surveys the apartment. Takeout containers are spread across the counters, and I'm suddenly self conscious of my temporary space as I take it in through someone else's gaze.

"No, I had to pick up two extra volunteer shifts, and spent an ungodly amount of time convincing my PR manager that it was in the best interest of the foundation for me to go to the wedding of the man supervising me at the hospital, all so I can do you this solid. One of those shifts I had to pick up is tonight, and I have to go in order to fulfill my contract hours. So, no, I don't have plans. They all changed the second I agreed to escort you to Jamaica at the last fucking minute." I point my glare in her direction, my tone slightly colder than I intended, but she's being a brat.

"Give me a fucking break, Cash. You're a grown ass man. If you didn't want to go, you would have said no."

I shrug her off, knowing she's right. "It's a cheap trip, only costs me airfare, since I'm staying with you. The price of the room barely changed, adding me on."

To be honest, the wedding part will suck, but being on the beach with unlimited food and drinks for this cheap is a straightforward decision. The bright blue eyes and full pink lips, icing on the cake. But, I won't let her know that, though. If she's going to be a brat, I can be one right back.

"Listen," I continue, "you want us to fight at the airport on the way home and break up, then we will have to have some distance and appear unhappy before then. I won't have to attend much of the festivities to make that plan work," I add sarcastically, knowing it's not something I would ever do.

"You *will* attend all the wedding festivities. We will do nothing on this trip to pull one ounce of attention from my brother and Blake," she demands.

We look at each other in a clear standoff for a few minutes before she grabs her purse and slings it over her shoulder. "Come on."

"Excuse me?" I ask.

"You're taking me to get coffee. It's our thing before you work long shifts. You want to make sure I'm good and caffeinated when you get home?" she says, wiggling her eyebrows.

"You gonna tell your mom and dad that little tidbit of information? Isn't that who the stories are for?"

She just gives me a pointed look and walks out the door.

I can't help but follow her. She has a magnetic pull that I can't escape.

"Black coffee? All the options on the menu, and that's what you order?"

I look over the edge of my cup at April, swirling her toffee nut latte with cinnamon and coconut milk. "I know what I like. There's no point in looking for something new when I have exactly what I want." I shrug.

"Humf," she scoffs, "you even drink coffee like a dick."

I chuckle and finally after a breath, I ask the one question I want the answer to.

"Why are you torturing yourself, April? Just tell your family we are not dating, and this entire charade can be over, or just tell them we broke up."

"Believe it or not, this is less torture, plus if I tell them we broke up, the entire trip will be spent grilling me about what happened, and I don't want the attention to be on that."

"Then stop being such a bitch to me, and put some effort into our fake relationship."

"Yeah, I'm the problem here." She rolls her eyes.

"You are," I deadpan before taking a sip of my coffee. "I'm doing you a favor, remember?"

She slowly raises her mug to her lips as if my words have no impact on her.

I follow the mug, tracing its path. The fullness of her lips highlights the glossy pink shade, making it pop. As the edge of the mug grazes her bottom lip, my stomach swirls. It slides across her delicate skin, pulling her lip open as she brings the mug back down to the table. When her tongue brushes against the drop of coffee lingering on her lip, and misses it, I can't help myself. I reach across the small table between us and swipe my thumb across her lip to retrieve the drop and slowly lick it off the pad of my finger.

She watches me intently as a small gasp leaves her mouth.

"So tell me a little about yourself, April? Why am I so obsessed with you?"

"Obsessed with me?" She scrunches her face.

"Absolutely. If you're going to be my girl, you will be *my* girl, my entire world."

She exhales as if she has been holding her breath and the more she talks, I almost think her walls are coming down slightly. "My love language is acts of service, and one way I enjoy spreading love is through food. I love to cook, but more than anything, I *love* to bake. There is nothing more welcoming than the smell of a warm treat in the oven, so I opened a bakery a while back. It's simple. I bake what sounds good that day, and it's what's on the menu, the only thing on the menu."

"You love acts of service, huh?" I chuckle, knowing the comment will get under her skin, but I'm growing to like the faint pink that blushes on her chest when she's irritated.

"Really, all that and you hang on the one thing you can turn dirty?"

"Chill out. I wanted to ruffle your feathers. I'm joking. How do customers handle the unpredictability?"

"They actually love it. I've learned that most people don't like making mundane decisions, so when they come to 'The Daily Bite' they don't have to choose. Plus the only item on the menu changes daily, keeping them excited for a surprise treat."

"Do they ever cycle back around?" I'm so intrigued by this idea.

"Of course they do. It's based on what sounds good to me at the moment. I have a few personal favorites that make a more regular appearance."

"Do you ever have someone come in hoping for something specific and leave disappointed?"

"Maybe, but I've never had a complaint. I have a box by the door where people can leave their requests for future visits. I call them crowd cravings. When I have one on the menu, I put it on the sign out front. That brings in a lot of curious business."

"Do you serve drinks?"

"Diner coffee, it's my favorite. Tried and true, predictable," she smiles, but I notice her shift uncomfortably in her seat. Almost like she is trying to remind herself she's supposed to be hating this.

"You just gave me shit about my coffee order, and that's what you serve?" I tease.

"I wanted a quick option for busy people. No need to fuss over your order, get in, get out. People love it."

"Get in, get out, huh?" I laugh,

"You are fucking impossible." She scoffs.

"People *do* love a quickie," I say with a cheeky smile.

She rolls her eyes, and I can't help myself. I wonder if they look that pretty rolling back in her head in ecstasy.

"Where are you taking me tomorrow?" she asks and that smile is back.

"You tell me. What would be your dream date? If we're telling stories, I want nothing but the best, but I have to be back in time for my night shift."

"My dream date would be a baking class, but more realistic maybe a day out shopping at a market or something."

"It's January, I don't know of any winter markets." I laugh.

"I said or something. Be creative, Cash."

"Find a class you want to take," I insist. I love how hot and cold she is today. It's better than just cold.

"Now?" she gasps. "If we book it at the last minute, it will cost a fortune."

"There is no cost too high for that sparkle in your eye," I respond, meaning every word, even if she thinks it a part of the act.

"Are you sure? This feels impulsive."

"100% sure."

She blushes, but pulls out her phone and starts looking.

"Ok, there is a 'Baking Around the World' class tomorrow, but it's too expensive, let me keep looking."

I hand her my card without questioning the amount.

"Absolutely not," she scolds. "We will split it. I'd offer to pay for both of us, if I thought I could afford it."

"Fine." I take my card back and set it on the table, simultaneously pulling out my phone and googling *Baking Around the World Class*. After a few seconds, our spots are reserved, and I put my phone back in my pocket and slide my card into my wallet.

"I'll pick you up at 8am."

She stares at my mouth agape, but doesn't say a word. She doesn't have to. It's written in her eyes. I'm guessing this is a class she's been wanting to take for a while. I didn't look at the cost, but the shine in her eyes is worth every penny.

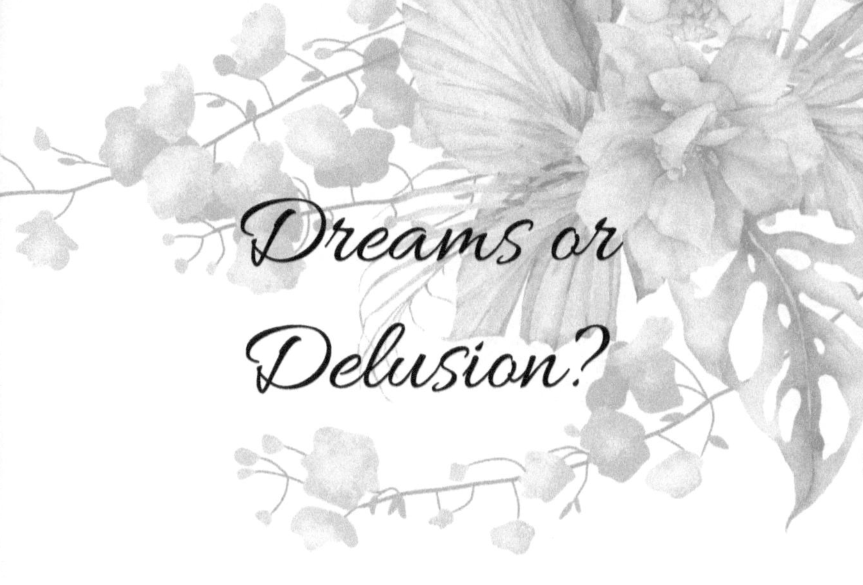

Dreams or Delusion?

"Somethin' in your voice caused me to turn my head"
-Kenny Chesney

April

"I LOVE THE SMELL in here, it reminds me of my grandma's house," Cash says as we walk into the baking class he signed us up for.

For the guy who breaks hearts, Cash has been awfully accommodating these last few days and seems really committed to getting to know each other so we can pull this whole fake relationship off. I'm not even sure why, because when we "break up" he will most likely come off like a piece of shit to my family and friends.

"Yeah, it reminds me of my grandma's, too. She always had fresh bread baking in the oven," I reminisce.

"What is your favorite bread?" he asks with a cautious glance over his shoulder as we settle up at our workstation, like he's not sure if people will recognize him.

"Well, I love to bake sourdough. There is just something so satisfying about the payoff that comes from such a lengthy process, plus a starter can really take on a personality of its own, ya know?" I smile, thinking about how much I love the process.

"Ummm… no. I actually don't know what you're talking about. What is a stater?" he chuckles.

"It's a bubbling little mixture of yeast, flour and water. You watch it for about two weeks and there should be little bubbles that dance about, showing off to let you know the yeast is alive. Then, you feed it and it matures. It's magical, Cash."

"So, it's moldy dough?" he asks, and my gasp is audible in the quiet room.

"You shut your mouth, Cash Easton," I whisper, trying not to call attention to the naivety of his comment in a room full of bakers.

He laughs and changes the subject. "What are we making today?"

"Ensaymadas. They're a buttery breakfast pastry topped with sugar and cheese. It's a staple in the Philippines."

"That actually sounds delicious." He rubs his hands together like a little kid waiting to win a prize, and I find myself wanting to see more of his charm.

"Once you get situated, there are directions on the recipe card. I will be around to assist as needed," the instructor calls out over the noise in the room.

I love advanced baking classes. They're more self-paced.

He leans over the card to read the instructions, and his face scrunches. "That's a shit ton of directions."

I laugh as I snatch the card and start setting up our yeast mixture. While we wait for the yeast to activate, we measure the dry ingredients.

I love every single thing about it. I reach for the flour and it dances around like dust in a breeze, little bits falling into the measuring cup like they know where to land. The sugar falls like delicate crystals, and the faint aroma of the two mixing in the air makes this unfamiliar kitchen feel like home.

I look up for the next ingredient and notice Cash sitting there staring.

"Don't get ahead of yourself, sitting there like a king waiting to be served. I know you're probably used to people waiting on you, but you're in this class too, sir. Get over here and give me a hand," I joke.

He smiles and starts reading the directions on the recipe card.

There is nothing better than getting lost in the kitchen. The aromas that fill the air wrap around like a comforting embrace, erasing every worry you may have. Baking is especially my favorite, calculated, controlled, and creative, just like me.

Before I know it, warm milk has mixed with all the dry ingredients, butter, and vanilla and it's time to add in the yeast mixture. When Cash hands it to me, I quickly realize how lost I got in the entire ordeal, ignoring him completely.

"Sorry. I just realized how engrossed I was in mixing everything together," I apologize with a shy smile.

"I was just as distracted. This is the first time I've gotten the pleasure of seeing pure joy on your face. It's much better than the disdain that usually paints your features when I'm around." He pushes a piece of fallen hair behind my ear. "Breathtaking."

That one word sends shivers up my spine, and I have to physically fight the reaction he has on my heart.

Why does he always have to say the exact right thing? And why does it make me want to run?

"Such a player." The words leave my lips with more distaste than I intended, but I can't get too close, so I let the tone linger.

"I was trying to pay you a compliment." His voice is equally full of scorn, and it makes my heart twist and turn, wishing I could make the words I feel come out of my mouth.

I know. I'm sorry.

After a long hour of silent baking, I bring a bite of the Ensaymada to my mouth. The warm Queso de Bola is such a salty contrast to the sugar coating on the top of the pastry, and I can't help but let a little moan leave my lips.

"Shit, this is delicious." I inhale deeply, taking in the savory smell that fills the air.

I startle and jump slightly when I feel the pad of Cash's finger dance across my bottom lip. When I look up, he is slowly bringing his thumb to his mouth, licking his finger clean.

"Sure is," he says, making such intense eye contact, I fold in on myself, trying to escape the heat. My body is betraying me at the moment, as I sit across from Cash, the definition of tall, dark, and handsome with piercing blue eyes. I see why women swoon, but his pretty face doesn't erase the douchebag tendencies, even though I have yet to really see them for myself. It causes me to question whether or not Blake really got an accurate picture of him the night of Knox and Ana's wedding.

I quickly push the thought aside, knowing how well Blake reads people, and giving myself a stern talking to.

Don't get drunk on his charm, April.

Not knowing what else to say, I ask, "Why are you looking at me like that?"

"Because that little taste was nowhere near enough, and I've never been good at restraint, it's taking more effort than I'd like to admit."

The look in his eyes makes it clear—he is not talking about the Ensaymada.

I feel my cheeks flush, and he notices. I know he does, because his gaze only gets more intense.

Shit, so much for not getting drunk on his charm, because if I'm honest, I've never been good at restraint either.

Cash

FUCK ME. WATCHING HER glide around our work station with pure joy is one of the sexiest things I have ever seen. The slight spring in her step each time she moves causes the golden locks she pulled into a high ponytail to bounce from side to side. She's bopping around humming an unrecognizable toon.

April is obviously attractive, with her hair, full lips, and subtle curves in all the right places. But to my surprise, it's not her looks that are drawing me in. It's everything about her. She is petite, but what she lacks in size, she makes up for in personality. She is direct, and passionate, and fuck, it's hot.

My dad always told me when I found someone who lived rent free in my mind, to make sure it's for more than her looks. *"There are millions of beautiful faces out there, but a limited number of beautiful souls. If you find someone who has both, you will feel like the richest man in the world, son."* I never truly believed my old man's words of wisdom until this very moment, when the face of an angel is secondary to the brightness she brings into my life, pain in the ass and all.

I already let my attraction to her slip, though I'm not sure she knows it's for real. Now that I've let my guard down and it's in motion, I'm going to have a hard time pulling back, so I need a defense mechanism to help me evade her. If I can't have fun *with* her, I'll have fun pushing her to the brink of wishing she could. By the end of this, she will want me too. I'll make sure of it. She'll wonder why in the hell she ever hated me to begin with. Maybe she'll even clue me in.

"I am not fucking you, Cash, I hate you." The words sound less convincing this time with a hint of a smile in her voice.

"We'll see sunshine. The veil between love and hate is mighty thin," I say with a wink.

"Not a veil when it's one dimensional, only hate." She rolls her eyes and takes another bite of her pastry, obviously trying to hide her smile.

Fuck, her mouth is pretty, with melty cheese dripping from her lips, spewing tough words. Bet it would be even better with something else falling in little drops.

The thought makes me shift, trying to find any sliver of control. Confessing my lack of restraint was no lie, and she is testing my limits as each dagger she throws my way has my cock stirring to life in my pants.

I grab a pastry from the tray and take a bite, and shit, it's just as good as she made it look.

"You should add these to the rotation. It will be a crowd craving for sure."

"That's the point of taking classes like this, Ace, you don't miss a thing." Her voice is full of sarcasm, yet accompanied by a smile as she continues, "But I honestly can't believe you remembered that small little detail about my shop."

"I've memorized every detail I can, Honey. You are an anomaly. Tiny as can be, with an attitude larger than life."

"Right, thanks for the reminder. We have to make this believable." To my surprise, her shoulders sag slightly at her false revelation. This little deal of ours has nothing to do with me internalizing every little detail. It's just the reason I get to.

"Or," I suggest, scooting closer. "Maybe I'm enjoying getting to know you better."

"Alright." She takes a deep, ragged breath. "Let's take a break from these shenanigans and get this cleaned up so you can take me home."

"Wow, that's a little fast, princess?"

"I fucking hate you," she glares, but it's not an angry glare like the ones I usually get. This one is forced.

The laugh that reverberates through my chest is the most genuine laugh I have had in a long time.

"Hand me the dishes," I insist. "I'll wash them while you finish your treat."

"I can do it," she says, attempting to grab the baking tray from my hands.

"Just because you can, doesn't mean you have to. Let me take care of it while you relax."

"Washing dishes will not make me like you," she deadpans.

"Well, maybe it will give you an opportunity to practice, because soon we have to appear to be a happy couple," I remind her.

"Shit," she stands, panic racing across her face.

"What?" I ask, looking around.

"I still know nothing about you, literally nothing," she says as she opens the notes app on her phone.

"What are you doing?" I ask as I rinse the soap from the pan.

"I'm taking notes so I can study them. I'll start with the things we have been doing."

She starts typing away on her phone mumbling as she adds to what, from here, looks like a list. "Breakfast dates, baking class…" She looks up at me clearly expecting me to add to this list of insanity.

"How did we start dating?" I ask, and she just stares at me, her eyes widening. "What?" I laugh.

"I have no fucking clue, Cash. I knew of you, but had never seen you in person before Blake's opening." She starts pacing, "I mean I don't really even know how big of a baseball star you actually are. For all I know, you might not even really play that much. I don't watch baseball."

Damn, she's cute when she panics.

"Ok, take a breath, Steamroller, and let's think about this logically—" She interrupts me.

"You gonna keep throwing out random nicknames until one sticks, or is this a kink thing?"

Brat. I internally smile.

She moves to add it to the list, and I put my hand on hers stopping her.

I look her straight in the eyes and keep talking, obviously ignoring her. "I spend a lot of time at the hospital where your brother works, The Daily Bite isn't far. I heard someone talking about it at the hospital, and I came in one day. The crowd's cravings caught my attention, which isn't a lie, I'm intrigued by it. I kept coming back, making it a once a week thing, and we just gradually started talking and slowly started catching feelings."

Maybe, also not a lie.

She takes a deep breath and her shoulders relax, "Ok, yeah, that sounds believable." She sits down next to me and starts a new list.

"Come on, tell me everything I need to know about you? Where are you from? What's your favorite color? Food? Anything a girlfriend would know." She is talking a million miles a minute again, and I decide trying to reason with her is pointless, so instead I decide to try and catch her off guard to settle her down.

I smirk, "Wings, the spicier the better, blue, Seattle, 9 inches and thick with a slight left curve." I wink.

She is tapping away at her phone, furiously taking notes, quietly repeating every word as she adds them to her phone.

"Seattle," she mumbles. "9 in," she pauses. "Right, maybe in your dreams, or delusions. Why does everything out of your mouth sound like the makings for a bad promo?" She rolls her eyes.

"Guess you'll never know, but an actual girlfriend would have every vein and ripple memorized." I shrug.

"How much of this bullshit is actually true, Cash? Knox will be there, remember? And he knows these things." Her voice is full of panic.

"What kind of friends do you think we are, sweet pea?" I raise a brow. "Knox most definitely does not know *all* of those things about me."

"You are impossible. This is a mistake." She sighs and leans on the counter with her head in her hands.

I move in behind her, caging her in between my arms as I whisper in her ear, "April, I promise you will not regret one second of this. I will make it worthwhile for you in every *fucking* way I can." My voice is full of fifty insinuations. "The only thing you will regret is not letting go and enjoying it."

I place a soft kiss on the side of her head, noticing the goosebumps peppering her skin before I return to the dishes on the counter.

Her mind and body are at odds. It's clear. I guess I'll have to give her a little more of myself, try to help her mind catch up, so maybe, just maybe, her heart will let go. As for mine, it's already crashing.

Reflections are Deceiving

"She looks great in cheap sunglasses, she looks great in anything"

-Brad Paisley

April

YESTERDAY SPIRALED FASTER THAN I could keep up. Cash doesn't take no for an answer, but I'm not looking to be just another notch on his bedpost.

I seek casual relationships, but the truth is, I've never had much experience, and being a virgin until 21 doesn't exactly prepare you for the world of no strings attached with a professional athlete. I've dated a lot, but I've only even been intimate with two guys: Knox, who didn't see me the way I needed him to, and Benji, the one I thought I'd share something real with.

He was the one I lost my virginity to, not because I was ready, but because I convinced myself I had to get it out of the way, with someone who mattered, even if I wasn't sure what that truly meant.

Always dramatic, I convinced myself I was missing out on something amazing, only to have the experience fall short every time, never come to completion. Guess you can't miss out on something you've never had.

The story of my life.

All that aside, I'm still human. And Cash? Well, the man is built like sin and scented like sex. Just looking at him makes me forget how little I actually like him.

As I finish packing my clothes into my suitcase, I keep replaying his voice in my head.

"Because that little taste was nowhere near enough, and I've never been good at restraint."

I shake off the feeling building between my legs and go to the bathroom to pack my essentials.

Distracted by the vision of his bright blue eyes, I aimlessly start placing items in my toiletry bag.

"Damn it," I groan as I lift the empty travel toothpaste.

"Guess I'm making a last minute trip to Walmart," I sigh in frustration because a trip to the store is the last thing I want to do.

I grab my purse and head to the store.

"Oh, my fuck!" I jump as I open the door. "Holy fucking fuck!" I yell, flailing my hands around in front of me as I step outside.

"What the hell is wrong with you?" Cash laughs.

"You scared the fuck out of me," I say as I slap him on the chest. "What the fuck are you doing here?"

"You know, if you keep asking me that, you're going to give me a complex."

"Well, stop showing up unannounced," I sneer.

"After I dropped you off yesterday, it occurred to me we should probably show up at the airport together, and if we were an actual couple, there would probably be something of mine you'd have to carry for me so I don't misplace or forget it. I lose everything, and Knox knows that."

"Ok…" I say, not knowing where he is going with this.

"I brought you my glasses. I wear them at night when I take my contacts out." Shit, Cash in glasses is probably sexy as hell.

"You couldn't give them to me in the morning?"

"I will probably forget them, because I set them aside to give to you. I forget shit, remember? Keep up, Slowburn." He smiles.

"Slowburn?" I scrunch my face in disapproval.

"Yeah, isn't that what they call it when things take forever to heat in a romance? I'm hot and ready, but you are taking time to warm up to the idea of us." He wiggles his brows.

I ignore him and push past him.

"Where are you going?"

"Walmart. I need toothpaste and mouthwash."

"Not quite the date I was envisioning, but we can make it fun," he laughs.

I scoff, wishing I could make this a quick trip, alone, but not fighting him when he ushers me to his car.

When we park, I scurry out of the car trying to find an escape from Cash's scent that is invading my head, fogging any rational thought I might have. His scent is a warm presence that is both comforting and alluring. The faint mix of amber and musk is sweet and sensual, creating an intoxicating sense of mystery and pure sex. Not allowing myself a second to fall prisoner to his allure, I walk as fast as I can to the front doors.

"Slow down, speed racer," he calls from somewhere behind me.

"Cash, we have to be at the airport early in the morning."

"Our flight leaves at 10. Slow down. What's wrong with you?"

"Nothing is *wrong* with me," I snap. "I just, I don't want… this. Whatever this is. Don't get used to it. Ok?" I try to convince myself more than I try to convince him.

He just stares at me for a moment with a hurt look on his face. Then, as if he didn't hear what I said, he continues, "Let's make shopping fun. We need snacks for the plane, so let's make a game of it."

"Snacks?" I question. "Are you 12?"

"I like to have a snack, and since I know you're off the table, I have to resort to prepackaged items."

"You are ridiculous," I say. "How is shopping for snacks fun?"

"We surprise each other with airplane approved snacks we think the other will like. The challenge is picking items you wouldn't usually pair together. The more specific our snacks are, the more it will appear we know about each other."

"Surprise, meaning we will not be shopping together?" I ask.

"Right. We surprise each other." He is unbothered by my sarcastic question.

"Well, at least I have a few minutes away from you."

Cash laughs, and as much as I want to convince myself that it's the truth, I'm starting not to mind his company.

He heads towards the clothes, weird, and I head towards the food. I wander around aimlessly for a few minutes trying to figure out what in the world to get him for this dumb game we are playing. Looking like a happy couple sure would be easier if I knew anything substantial about him. Too bad I'm not interested in learning anything about the dickhead who hurt my friend.

"Jerky and seeds. He plays baseball. Those sound like baseball approved snacks." I give myself a proverbial pat on the back and throw them into my cart.

Now for the shit I came here for. I make my way around the store to the travel toiletry section and grab the few essentials I was missing. Alright, now I can go home and, shit. We're sharing a room.

It dawns on me that I don't own pajamas. One who lives on their own and sleeps in the nude, well underwear, wouldn't need them.

This is going to be miserable. There are few things I hate more than sleeping with clothes on. They get all bunched up and twist, it's so uncomfortable. Plus waking up in sweat-drenched clothes is not a sensation I'm fond of. Every time I have tried to sleep in even a tight fitting tank, I either wake up a hundred times a night, or mindlessly shed them.

Looks like I have one more stop to make on my way to the register.

Fucking Cash.

Cash

I FOLLOW APRIL INTO the store, and I can't help but smile at how flustered she gets when I'm so direct about my attraction to her.

She clearly hates me, and I can't figure out why she hasn't broached the conversation about what happened with Blake and I. You'd think she would want nothing more than an opportunity to put me in my place.

Luke and I had a good conversation at the hospital, and I was able to clear some shit up, so I'm at a loss as to why exactly she hates me so much.

Maybe I shouldn't have expected he'd talk to her about it. He probably assumes she already knows, since we're "dating." I don't know how to bring it up without her thinking I'm spewing bullshit so I'll just have to win her over with my charm.

When we hit the door, she heads straight for the grocery department, while I turn left. She moves quickly as if being in my proximity pains her.

I have watched her intently in the little time we have spent together and have made a note of a few specific things. She loves sweets, and caffeine. Knowing it's going to be a long day, I opt for protein. I get a box of blueberry muffin protein bars, and a box of tropical liquid IV packets with caffeine. Maybe it's the athlete in me, but hydration is essential, especially when traveling.

April strikes me as the sunbathing type, and one thing I'm positive she can use is a sunscreen lip balm. Last time I traveled to Jamaica with my family, we all left with burnt lips, so I add two to the cart.

I spend the next fifteen minutes walking around the store, trying to find the feisty little blond that is stealing my heart. She is such a pain in the ass, and I love it.

On my third lap around the store, I spot a tiny little figure peeking out from the clothes rack closest to the register.

I stand back and watch her for a minute. Her face is scrunched, and she's frantically sifting through the garments displayed in the rack in front of her. If looks could kill, those pajamas would be dust.

"What are you looking for, cupcake?" I say as I walk up behind her and lean in to whisper in her ear. "I was thinking you left me here."

"I wish," she says as she runs her fingers over a set of sleep shorts. She makes a disgusted look and then grabs the same sleep set in another color and places them in the cart.

"Why are you getting those if you clearly don't like them?"

"I like them just fine. They're cute, but I usually sleep naked, and when I was getting the stuff I needed, I realized *you* will sleep in my room," she says the word you like it's sugar laced poison.

"Well, don't feel you need them on my account. I fully support you sleeping in the nude."

She rolls her eyes, her usual little reaction to my antics.

"Let's check out. I still have to finish packing," she sounds obviously annoyed, cutting our conversation short.

We walk to the register and she places the items from the cart onto the conveyor belt.

"I got it," I say as she reaches for her purse.

"No," she answers flatly.

"I want to," I insist as the cashier scans the items.

"Seeds? All the snack options in the store, and you got sunflower seeds?" I ask sarcastically.

"You play baseball, right?" Her tone has a clear edge to it, as if I'm an idiot for not connecting the dots she's laying down.

"Yes…" I answer hesitantly.

"Well, baseball players are always eating seeds." She looks me dead in the eyes like I am indeed an idiot.

"Sweetheart, you can't spit seeds on the plane. I mean, I love seeds, but not on an airplane."

"Well, I don't know what you like, and this game is dumb. You can have some of whatever you got me." Her irritation is so sexy.

The cashier is staring at a hole in my profile, and is jittery as he waits for a lull in our conversation. I know the feeling buddy, she makes it hard to get a word in.

"You're Cash Easton." His post pubescent voice jumps a few octaves. "Holy shit, I saw you walk by and told myself no way that's him. We're too far from Cali, but then I heard her say you play, and shit! You're Cash Easton."

I take a glance at his name tag, "How are you, Ricky?" I ask as I place the rest of my items on the conveyer.

"Really good now. This is the highlight of my shift."

"You play ball?" I ask.

He struggles to scan the items, but I don't mind. I would have lost my shit if I would have been face to face with a professional athlete at his age.

"Yeah, since I was old enough to hold a bat."

"Are you graduating soon?"

"This year," he responds, dropping the box of protein bars.

"That's awesome. Any plans for college ball?"

"Just committed to Virginia Tech." He smiles.

"Shit man, go Hokies. What position you play?" This is a pretty cool kid.

"Catcher."

"Great position if you wanna go pro. You can never have too many catchers." I finish putting the bags in the cart. "You know, I'm here off and on for some volunteer work. When you get home, follow me on Insta. Maybe we can do some training together when I'm in town."

"Shit. Really?" He gives me a look like he can't believe the words coming out of my mouth.

"Yeah, I need to be better at training while I'm here, and having a partner will hold me accountable."

"Thanks." Ricky responds, trying to play it cool, but his smile betrays him. Anyone close by could tell he's shocked this is actually happening.

"Talk to you soon, Ricky."

April watches as I push the cart, her eyes following my every motion.

"You just made that kid's whole life." I swear I see the faintest of smiles cross her expression.

"Maybe. He seemed like a cool kid, and if he's playing D1, he's serious about the game."

"That's sweet, Cash."

Holy shit, am I making progress? She might actually not hate me.

Last Minute Preparations

"Sometimes I thank God, for unanswered prayers,"
-Garth Brooks

April

I DIDN'T SLEEP A wink last night. By the time Cash dropped me off and I finished packing, my brain was wide awake, buzzing with thoughts I shouldn't be having. It felt like a blender whirring inside my skull, all the gears grinding in overdrive. I couldn't switch it off.

Similar sounds swirl around me as the airport bar hums with the sound of the margarita machine whirring, spinning ice and alcohol into a slushy mess. I stare at the thick, swirling contents, my mimosa barely touched in my hand. Two things I know about this trip: I need to calm down or I'll never sleep, and I need a constant flow of alcohol to get through the day.

Cash picked me up at 7:30 so we could settle in before the others arrived for our 10 a.m. flight. It's now 9:32, and I'm on my third mimosa, but my nerves still itch like they're on fire. Cash ducked out to the restroom and when he comes back we'll head over to the gate.

I spin the stem of my mimosa glass between my fingers as I contemplate my actions.

I thought this was a good idea. Why? I couldn't tell you. But up to now, I was sure it would work. I imagined us playing the perfect couple, leaving Blake and Luke to enjoy their honeymoon while we staged a breakup. Simple. Clean. No problem. Shit, now I have real feelings, and my fake boyfriend is nothing but charming.

I also didn't account for the fact I would be with *Cash Easton*, a sports legend that makes people stop in their tracks. Rick, the cashier, should have been my first clue into his life as a star athlete, but I was too distracted by my swirling brain to register the extent of his fame.

As soon as he stepped away this morning to use the restroom, I saw it: no less than five people swarmed him, asking for pictures and autographs. I've been here ever since, head down, eyes trained on the table, dodging the phones aimed in my direction. 'Cash Easton's arm candy'. That's me now.

"He is so hot. Where do you think they're going?" a woman behind me asks her friends.

"Probably a secluded place to have alone time. What else would you do with a man like that?" one of her friends responds with a suggestive tone in her voice, as if I'm sixty feet away and can't hear them, instead of less than three.

"She must be a hookup, I haven't heard that he has a girlfriend."

The assessment of our situation makes my skin crawl, as it's not the persona I want floating around where I'm concerned. Even if it is from a group of women I've never seen and never will again. I find myself aching to preserve my reputation.

I literally want to turn around and give them a piece of my mind, but my attention is quickly diverted to Cash.

"You ready, daydreamer?" he asks as he lays money down on the bar for our drinks, placing a soft kiss to the side of my head.

"I guess," I sigh, grabbing my purse and suitcase and making my way to the door of the small restaurant instead of engaging in a hen fight.

"Why didn't you check your bag?" he asks.

"I'm already sharing a room with you. No need to risk making this trip worse by having to wear the same clothes all week because my bag gets lost." I huff. "I never check my bags on a connecting flight."

"You fit all your shit in that bag?" he asks skeptically.

"Sure did. This isn't my first rodeo."

He smiles and takes the handle of my bag, wheeling it to the gate for me.

"You don't have to do that," I say.

"No, I don't, but I told you, if you are mine, you are all mine. I treat women I date like a fucking princess." He whispers, "Knox knows that."

"Right," I inhale deeply.

We continue walking to the gate, and I can't wait to find a corner to fall into and hide. Every time I look up there are phones pointed in our direction.

"I didn't know there were this many Sun Cats fans in Vermont." I try to hide my face, but it's no use. They're coming from all directions.

"There aren't. Most of them probably don't even follow the team, and some of them probably even hate the team, but sports fans alike will go to the ends of the Earth to prove they had a close encounter with a player." He seems so unfazed as he puts his arm around me and pulls me in close. It's a clear attempt to shield me from the onlookers, and I appreciate the effort.

As we approach the gate, I see Luke and Blake standing near the check-in desk, talking. I quickly survey the space and realize they're the only ones here. My heart rate picks up, bile rising in my throat.

"Wait," I say, pulling Cash back.

He quickly lets go of the bag handle and turns so he is blocking my view of Luke and Blake. He reaches out and frames my face with his calloused hands. The faint scent of amber and musk evades my senses.

"Look at me." He leans in so his breath is a whisper away, "This is not how I expected to spend my week either, but you are the most amazing woman I have ever met. I mean it." He wraps me in his arms, whispering in my ear. To anyone nearby, we look like two people madly in love. "I have watched you in your element memorizing every detail possible, and the sight is breathtaking, Angel. Believe me when I say nothing about my admiration is an act."

I pull away slightly so I can see his ocean eyes and smile when I am met with nothing but sincerity.

"Stop fighting this, April." He tucks a hair behind my ear. "We're too far in for bailing now. We might as well have fun on this trip. They already think we're together, so the only one this little show of resistance is for, is *you*."

He grabs my hand and leads me towards my brother and Blake, who are whispering as we approach.

As soon as we are close enough to hear their hushed conversations, Luke pulls me into a hug. Blake offers a cordial greeting to Cash and gives me a hug, pulling me in tight.

"There is my little ray of sunshine," my dad's voice booms over the crowd. He is walking towards us with a big smile on his face. I love knowing I can always count on my parents' perfect timing in tense situations.

"Hi daddy. This is Cash. Cash, this is my dad."

"Nice to meet you, Mr. Jennings." Cash offers his hand to my dad.

Without hesitation, my dad pulls Cash into a bro hug, patting his back. "Call me Matt. Nice to, officially, meet you, Cash. Mags come meet Cash," he yells over to my mom.

"Oh, Cash, it's so nice to meet you!" my mom's words drip like honey.

I can do this, I encourage myself.

After everyone has gotten acquainted, and some of the tension has dissipated. Cash excuses himself to run and grab coffee before we board. Mom and dad accompany him, so I address the elephant in the room with Blake and Luke.

"I really don't want this to be uncomfortable. Are you ok?" I ask Blake.

"Yes, Ap, you're the only one making this awkward." She smiles.

Luke pipes in, "Sis, we're good."

"How are you, good? You punched him, Blake hated him, and suddenly we're all just ok with this?" I let out a little laugh but not because it's funny, because what I really want to do is scream.

Blake reads my expression, "It was a misunderstanding."

I feel the confusion on my face and quickly shift to divert my eyes to someone walking by.

"You talked to Cash?" I look between them genuinely wondering, but feeling like the question is safe enough for the situation that won't give me away, because right now I have no fucking clue what they are talking about.

"Cash approached me one day at the hospital and explained everything," Luke says.

"Ok?" My voice is low and it's clear I want him to elaborate.

"When he said she wasn't worth the hype, he was talking about a new bat he bought and Blake thought he was talking about her." He coughs in his hand, clearly not wanting to acknowledge the fact that Cash and Blake hooked up.

"To be fair, he was referring to the bat as *she* and I was already feeling a little wounded," Blake cuts in.

"Who the hell refers to a bat as *she*?" I ask, trying to catch up.

"Apparently it's a baseball thing." Blake rolls her eyes.

"He seemed pretty bummed he lost his shot." Luke leans in and gives Blake a kiss on the forehead, not even realizing he's talking about my "boyfriend."

"I— Are you sure? You believe him?" I ask, confusion marred across my face.

"He seemed pretty torn up. I mean, I don't blame him for being jealous, but I'm glad you thought he was a prick." He laughs again in Blake's direction, "Otherwise, who knows, when I ran into you, you might have been off the market."

"Why are you looking at us like all of this is new news?" Blake questions. "You knew this already. Otherwise you wouldn't have started seeing him right?" Shit, I'm letting the truth show.

"Yes, B. I just want to make sure you really believe him, and you're not just pretending for me," I strain, trying to make my voice sound irritated, to hide the truth.

My body heats and I fold into myself, trying to disappear. Embarrassment taking over. Here I am sitting across from my brother and his fiancée, who my "boyfriend" is in love with.

Jealousy. Why am I feeling jealous? That bitch has terrible timing.

Cash

"THERE IS JUST SOMETHING about her. I can't put my finger on it, I really like her. But, she's irritated as hell with me right now." Knox and April have history, so I figured he'd be the best one to get advice from, to help me get in her good graces. I made a beeline for him the second I came back after giving April her coffee.

"April's a sweet girl. She was there for me when I found out I couldn't play baseball anymore. She's good for you," he says.

"Why didn't you two work out if she's so amazing?" My curiosity takes over.

"She's not Ana. That's really all it came down to."

I'm not sure anyone loves another person more genuinely than Knox loves Ana.

"How do I get back on her good side?" I ask.

"Fuck if I know, I was never on her bad side. But I bet you have your work cut out. She's stubborn as hell."

He laughs, adding, "She doesn't seem that mad. What did you do?"

"Beats me. She puts up a good front when everyone's around."

Movement to my right steals my attention, and there is no getting it back.

April is walking over to the seats in front of the gate, coffee in hand and a stoic look on her face. It guts me. All I want her to be is the bubbly piece of perfection I've seen from her when she's in her element. I want to be a part of her element, a safe place to be herself, and relax. She can be so bright, but right now, her light's dimmed, and I hate it.

I don't even finish my conversation with Knox. I walk towards her without a word, as if there is a magnetic pull moving me in her direction.

"Do you want something small to eat before we board?" My words seem to have fallen away from her ears before they reached them, because she just continues to stare at her phone.

I take my index finger and curl it under her chin to guide her gaze in my direction.

"You ok, sweetheart?"

"Yeah, sorry." She shakes her head as if to clear away a thought she's lost in. "What were you saying?"

"Do you want to grab something small to eat before we board?"

"No, we have all the snacks we packed." She offers me a smile, but it seems forced.

"We are now boarding group A..." the voice over the speakers breaks the silence between us, but I can't seem to focus on the rest of the announcement. Her honey blond hair swaying with each small motion is stealing my attention.

Fuck she's beautiful.

The first time I met April she was in a black cocktail dress and pink, high-heeled ankle boots that matched her plump lips perfectly. Her shoulder length blond hair was swaying in the wind. She was a vision. Every moment I have spent with her since then, she's flawlessly put together, dainty gold jewelry and all.

Today she is in a cream sweatsuit with tan tennis shoes, and while she is a more relaxed version of herself, she's still completely put together. Nothing rattles her, so this sudden change in demeanor is worrying me. I should have pushed harder for her to tell her family the truth. I shouldn't have been so consumed with getting to spend time with her. She is frayed and ruffled around the edges, and it's not her.

"Let's go." She smiles, but it's not bright.

"Ok." I grab her bag and lead her to the line with my hand glued to her lower back. The touch feels instinctive, like it's always been this way, a quiet connection between us. There's an unspoken comfort in the simple motion, a subtle rhythm that flows naturally, as though we've done this countless times before. A part of me wants to know how this would feel in 20 years.

We wait in line silently for them to call boarding group C, and each time she moves, the smell of brown sugar fills my senses.

When we finally step onto the airplane, the only seats available that are together are at the back, just a few rows from the last.

"Oh hurry, get that row." She shoves me forward a little to quicken my step as if someone in the line behind us might launch over us and take them. "I hate the very back row. The seats don't recline."

I laugh. "There's no one in front of us, Tizzy. I think we're safe to choose whichever seats we want back here."

She ignores my playful response and continues to push me forward.

"Which seat do you want?"

"I love the window. It's like a built-in headrest when I doze off." She climbs inside and sets her gigantic purse on the floor in front of her.

I turn to inspect the line behind us, and realize there is absolutely no way we will have a row to ourselves, so I cram my 6'4" frame in the middle seat beside her.

"Cash, no," she sighs. "I'm sorry. I wasn't thinking. This is almost a 3 hour flight. Move to the aisle," she demands.

"I'm not letting someone else sit between us for 3 hours," I protest.

"I wasn't suggesting someone sit between us. Scoot over so I can move. I'll sit in the middle so you can sit on the aisle." Her tone is not very amused, yet warm.

After she and the woman who now occupies the window seat got settled, I secured her bag in the overhead bin and picked a movie we could watch together.

I pulled up "The Proposal" on my iPad, and handed her one of my earbuds.

"I love this movie." There's that smile I adore so much. "Betty White is hilarious, dancing around, singing in the woods. Oh, but my favorite scene is when Sandra Bullock comes running out of the bath-room and they topple to the floor naked."

She's already cracking up and the opening credits are still rolling.

If this is what watching movies with April is like, I want to do a hell a lot more of it.

"What made you pick this movie?" she asks.

"Well," I lower my voice to a whisper and lean in close to her ear so my words only fall on her.

"I figured we could do a little homework before we land. They made fake dating work."

She smiles in approval, and it makes being crammed in an airplane seat feel like the best place to be.

As we watch the movie, April giggles at all the funny parts, and the sound is pure perfection.

I can tell she's getting tired as the bonus scene during the credits roll. She shifts uncomfortably, trying to find the perfect position between me and the woman to her right.

I pull the armrest up and pull her into my side.

"What are you doing?" Her eyes go wide and she pulls away slightly to look me in the eyes.

"Well, I guess it's a good thing everyone else we know is sitting up front." I smirk. "I'm letting you use me as a pillow."

I pull her back towards me, only this time she doesn't fight it.

She lays her head on my shoulder and cuddles up into my embrace, pulling her legs up to her chest. She is so tiny, she fits perfectly.

After a few minutes, she dozes off. The low rumble of the plane fills the space between us, steady and calming. I feel the weight of her breath against my skin, and before long, I'm following her into the quiet, the world outside forgotten for a while.

When The World Tilts On Its Axis

"Talkin' would take too much time"

-Riley Green

April

"U fff," I wince as I raise my head from Cash's shoulder. I'm not sure exactly how long I was asleep, but despite the crick in my neck from the awkward position, it's the best sleep I've gotten in a while, and we're on a plane, so there's that.

I resettle my position, and look at Cash. He's still sleeping, his dark lashes dancing with each breath. He is a beautiful man. I noticed his good looks the first time I laid eyes on him, but it was tainted by the person I believed him to be, but now…

He's Cash.

I lean back on my seat taking in the version of him I have been with for the past few days in preparation for this trip.

The man who agreed to be my "boyfriend" with far less protest than I was expecting.

The man who took me on dates to build a believable fake relationship before we came here.

The man who comforted me to sleep on a plane, who was willing to squeeze his tall frame into the middle seat without hesitation knowing he'd be miserable on a long flight so I would be comfortable.

Cash fucking Easton, a pro baseball player who could have any women in the world is here with me, and I'm fighting it.

Why?

I hated him when I thought he hurt Blake, but now that I know the truth, all I am is jealous, because somewhere behind all the hate, he won me over without me even knowing it.

The sting of the realization that he really wanted to be with Blake is a sharp, sudden sensation that catches me off guard, leaving a lingering ache. It's like a quick jolt. A tiny bee sting where the initial impact is intense and surprising, but as it settles in, it fades to a dull, persistent throb.

"What are you doing awake, Hummingbird?" he asks with a sleep coated smile, and my insides churn to life.

"Just thinking."

"About?" he asks.

"Bee stings," I respond not knowing what else to say.

"Interesting," he chuckles.

"My neck is stiff like when I got stung by a bee as a kid." I smile, but the lie makes it soft and forced.

He notices, because the second I try to avoid his gaze, he reaches out and forces my eyes to meet his with the gentle pressure of his curled index finger below my chin.

Not a word is spoken between us. The silence is filled by the charge of his piercing blue eyes mirroring my own.

"Has anyone ever told you how much you look like Giacomo Giannotti?" I blurt the words almost as fast as the thought crosses my mind.

"Is that the doctor from Grey's anatomy?"

I nod, confirming he's correct.

"I've heard it a few times, mostly from reporters who want to win me over with flattery during interviews."

I nod again, swallowing with a tight smile. I'm still unsure how to deal with the rollercoaster of emotions being next to him brings. I pull my Beats from my bag and slide them over my ears.

He gives me a puzzled look, but I avoid his stare.

After a few moments of me listening to music, I feel the heat of his stare burning through me. My insides are an inferno. Because when Cash Easton stares at you like you are the only one in the room, your body has no choice but to react, to betray you.

My attempt to convince myself that this is a natural reaction and not my feelings getting in the way is futile.

Shit! I clench my thighs together, furious that my body won't get on board with my brain. I need air. I need space, I need a fucking lifeboat.

I stand abruptly, trying to get the cool air from the tiny fucking little stream of air overhead to hit me. Only problem is that Cash's large frame causes his legs to block me.

"Can you move?" My words are sharp and abrupt.

"Sure?" He looks at me with a concerned look.

"I have to pee." I have to get out of here, away from him for a few minutes.

He stands so I can exit the seats, but he doesn't move far, his presence blocking my path so I have to squeeze past him, our arms graze and I shudder at the contact.

Moments later, I'm standing in the bathroom trying to cool the fuck down and reason with myself in the tiny clouded mirror as I run ice cold water over my wrists.

"You can't have him, April. He is not who you think he is. He has women falling at his feet," I whisper to myself, ensuring I have steady eye contact across the glass.

You're wrong. What's stopping you?

I shake my head, attempting to shake the thoughts loose as I splash cold water on my face. The icy droplets sting my skin, a sharp contrast to the heat burning behind my eyes. I let out a shaky breath, trying to clear my mind, but the words echo relentlessly. *He really wishes you were Blake.*

I stare at my reflection in the mirror. The water dripping down my face like unwanted tears.

I can't be who he wants.

With a frustrated sigh, I wipe my face and step back from the sink. The room feels too small, the air too thick. I don't have time for this.

Cash

April was gone way longer than necessary, unless she had a sudden case of the runs, or was avoiding my glare as she ignored me. I'm betting on the latter.

She came back and has been sitting with her headphones listening to music, or a book, who knows what for the past five minutes, and is playing with the frayed edges of her sweater as it sits on her lap.

Her entire demeanor shifted right before we loaded the plane, and I don't know her well enough to read the reaction, but I'm going to make it my mission to memorize every expression that crosses her face.

But right now, she is frustrating the shit out of me.

"April," I whisper. "April."

Nothing.

I tickle her side and she jolts, but still doesn't respond.

Unable to take the silence for one more second, I pull out my phone and type a message on my notes app. It's too quiet to have a full blown conversation, and I'm not sure if she purchased the WiFi to text.

Me: What happened?

I hand her the phone, waiting for her response, but all she does is shake her head and mouth the word "nothing" and then goes back to her music or whatever she's listening to.

Me: April, please. What happened?

She huffs out a breath and pecks at the phone typing her response before shoving it back at me.

Her: I'm tired.

I roll my eyes.

Me: Cut the bullshit, that's what women say when they either don't want to talk about something, or don't want to fuck.

She scoffs typing out her response, but this time we go back and forth for a beat.

Her: You fell for Blake?

Me: What? No!

Her: Sure.

Me: Wait! Are we fighting?

Her: Yes, you embarrassed me.

Me: What? When?

Her: My brother said you liked Blake and the entire conversation at the cafe was a misunderstanding.

Me: It was. I thought I liked her, but that was before I knew you.

Her: Typical response.

"The fuck?" I whisper.

Me: April, look at me.

I flash her the phone and make sure her eyes stay locked on me so she sees me before she reads my next response.

Me: I'm tired of all the bullshit that comes with being an athlete like girls throwing themselves at me. I want something real for once, and my optimistic side thought I found that with her, but I fucked that up before I even got the chance to know her. It sucked, but I wasn't heartbroken. I didn't even chase her when she left. I just let her go, so I knew we weren't meant for each other. When you showed up at my apartment, everything clicked. The thought of you coming here alone was a reality I couldn't accept.

She instantly rolls her eyes.

Me: I mean it. I like you, Tulip. I'm sorry you got embarrassed.

Her: It's fine.

Me: Don't do that. Don't shut down. Talk to me.

Her: We're typing out messages, that's hardly talking.

Me: You know what I mean. You're mad, not just embarrassed. Help me understand so I can make it better.

She thinks about it for a second before responding.

Her: I was jealous. Despite the fact that I thought you were a piece of shit, I still really liked spending time with you. And that also makes me mad at myself. I was a bad friend. I fell for you even though I thought you were a shitbag to my best friend.

Her admission sends butterflies dancing in my stomach, and I can't fight the smile.

Me: So… you're saying there's a chance?

She laughs, startling the women beside her.

"Sorry," she winces.

She turns to say something as the captain comes over the speaker.

"We are starting our final descent. We'll be landing in ten minutes. Please make sure your belongings are stowed under your seats, and your seats are in the upright position. Welcome to Florida."

Well, on the first leg of this trip we actually had an honest conversation. I wonder what will come from the second?

It takes more like 30 minutes to land and taxi in, and I spend the entire time plotting various ways I can crack her shell, and make her see me for who I am.

I'm starting to realize that maybe she's not great at communicating through direct conversations, the conversations we had via my notes app was the first real conversation we've had where I felt like we were actually getting somewhere.

Once we reached the gate and cleared us to exit the plane, I grabbed her bag and followed her up the aisle.

"How long is our layover?" I wonder aloud.

"Just long enough to pee and grab some coffee. Maybe 40 minutes, but we will start reloading the plane in about 15." Her tone is sleepy and quiet.

"You go pee, I'll grab the coffee," I insist.

As soon as we reach the end of the walkway, she sprints towards the restroom and I make my way to the coffee stand nearby, but I stop in my tracks when I notice a little diner style restaurant on the way.

I peek in for a second. "Can I order coffee to go?" I ask the hostess.

"Yes, just walk up to that window, and the lady in red can help you." Her smile is bright and cheery.

A few minutes later I have two diner coffees in paper cups with cream and sugar, and a honey packet just in case.

I walk up to the gate and April is already in line visiting with Ana and Blake.

"Here you go, Tulip," I say, handing her the warm paper cup carefully wrapped in a paper towel. "It's from that little diner, so they didn't have sleeves. Be careful."

She offers me a slight sign of appreciation accompanied by a soft smile.

"Diner coffee." Her smile morphs into a loving pout and slight tilt of her head and she looks at me.

"And he got honey, smart man," Blake adds, smiling at me indicating how much she approves of my gesture for her friend.

"Thank you," April raises to her tiptoes and places a soft kiss to the tip of my nose.

"We thought it would be fun for us to sit together on this flight so we can make plans for our girl's night out on the resort. Are you ok sitting with the guys?" she asks me.

"Of course," I lie. And when she walks away, all I can think about is the space she's leaving behind.

Confusion

"And I'm too vain to kiss in the rain.."

-Kelsea Ballerini

April

"Ok, Knox insists he is a great guy, and goes on and on about how much he spoils girls he's dated, but that was so cute!" Ana says in a sing-song voice as we situate our things on the plane.

"Kids have made you extra mushy." Blake laughs, nudging Ana's shoulder with her own. "Where are my badass friends who don't take shit and find mushy love a little overrated?"

"I'm a few months postpartum, my mother-in-law graciously volunteered to stay with the kids, and this is the first vacation I've taken in a long time, Blake. I'm about to be the mushiest love sick bitch you've ever met." Ana laughs.

"Ok, what are we doing on our night out?" Blake asks, and I find myself relieved by the change in subject.

It was cute that he remembered how much I love diner coffee and opted for that in place of a latte from the coffee stand, but no one else knows exactly how much it rattled me, because to the rest of them it appears as a thoughtful gesture from a loving boyfriend. To me though, it's more than that. It's the idea that he remembered that little detail from our conversation a few days ago. It's the idea that he listens, cares, and memorizes every detail. That little gesture is way beyond the expectations of a fake boyfriend, but one of someone who truly cares.

Maybe I need to actually start listening to the words he's saying and stop writing my own narrative. I hate that I've done to him what everyone does to me—jumping to conclusions and assuming his intentions.

Refocusing on the conversation, I chime in, "Do you want a relaxing day, or an unhinged day?"

"Let's find a happy medium. I don't want to be hung over for the wedding." Blake scrunches her face in thought. "I'd really love to sit in a cabana by the beach and read, and then maybe get a low key lunch, and then at night maybe hit a bar or two on the resort and sing karaoke."

"That sounds amazing." Ana smiles at Blake, "The guys are golfing, right?"

"Yes, and then they are going on a dinner catamaran. They won't be back until later in the evening."

"Catamarans are so much fun!" I added. "We went on one on our family vacation, and the food was incredible."

"Oh, I heard the resort has a sushi restaurant. I've been wanting sushi." Ana lets a soft little moan escape her mouth.

"Easy," Blake laughs, "I love sushi, but I'm not down for listening to you make sex noises over it."

The guys are a few rows in front of us, across the aisle, and Cash is sitting in the end seat giving me the most delicious view of his veiny, olive forearm propped up on the armrest.

He is deep in conversation with the guys, and every time he moves, the veins protrude just a little more. I find myself missing being wrapped up in his firm grip while I snoozed on the last flight.

"So what do you and Luke have planned for your honeymoon, leaving out all of the spicy details?" I ask, trying to distract myself from the gorgeous man a few rows up.

"We are staying at the same resort. We were going to move, but it felt like such a hassle, so we invested the money we were saving into fun things to do. We have a couples' massage one day, and a few excursions planned, mostly just relaxing and enjoying each other's company." Thank fuck she gave me the PG version.

"I want the extended version of that story later, when little sister ears are not around," Ana teases tilting her eyes dramatically in my direction. She is a sucker for all the smutty details.

"Is there really anything that fabulous to share about sex?" I genuinely wonder out loud trying to cover the fact that my body just won't let me get there. "It just feels like a means to an end for the guy, you know?"

"Um…" Ana chuckles. "No, I definitely do not know."

The look on her face is pure befuddlement.

"You still haven't had an O?" Blake asks, accidentally raising her voice, but still not loud enough to get Cash's attention. I look in his direction to make sure of it.

"Shhh…." I scold, "No, I haven't."

"I know you don't have a lot of experience, but not even with Cash?" she questions me, clearly not believing a word I'm saying. "I mean, shit, he gave me one, and I'll emphasize *one* of the most mind numbing orgasms of my life."

She stares at me mouth agape. "Sorry, I didn't mean to make that awkward. The words just came out."

"We haven't been intimate." I can feel the heat radiating off my face, as my cheeks flush with my confession. Luckily the girls know me well enough not to make me feel worse about it.

"You have never, not one time, had an orgasm?" Ana pipes in, her voice barely a whisper. Clearly she has not made the connection that one of the few men I have been intimate with, sans climax, is her husband.

"I don't think so," I answer, honestly.

"Oh you would know." She wiggles her brows.

"Wait…" There it is, realization written all over her face. "Does Knox know you didn't finish, I can't imagine him letting that slide." Ana's voice is even lower this time.

I give her a pained look, this conversation is taking a very uncomfortable turn.

"Oh, please April." She shoos my thoughts away with a flick of her wrist. "Knox was a fuckboy, you think I don't know that? But," she tilts her head as she thinks. "It makes me feel a little bit better that sex between you two blew chunks."

A loud laugh leaves my mouth, and this time we definitely catch Cash's attention.

"This is embarrassing. I can't believe we are having this conversation. Plus, we are toxic as fuck," I point out.

"We're just living our best dramatic TV show lives, everyone did everyone, get over it." Ana laughs.

"More important than our tangled pasts, we need to help you finish." Blake's voice is low and serious.

"Um… pass. I don't know what that even means." The red returns to my face.

"Not helping you in a physical way. April, you have to let go, clear your mind and only focus on the sensations," Blake explains.

"You also have to ask for what feels good." Ana adds, "It's about you too, not just him," and laughs.

"I don't even know what I like," I admit.

"Then you have to pay better attention and learn."

"Learn?"

"Yes, have you ever, you know?" Ana asks, looking down.

"No," I say in surprise. "I never have the desire."

"Girl, you have no idea what you're missing." Blake knows me better than most, so I'm surprised by how shocked she is by this information.

I literally have no libido. But, lucky me, the remainder of the flight was spent giving me strategic advice on how to achieve the "best feeling" in the world.

Cash

I MISSED HER, AND I didn't even expect to. It hit me out of nowhere. She was right there the whole flight, close enough to hear her voice, but somehow, I spent the last three and a half hours missing her.

I could hear her faint laughter, her soft voice, and the occasional things she'd say a bit too loud. Still, something about it felt different. It was like there was a quiet space between us that I couldn't quite fill, even though she was so close.

I didn't pay much attention to the conversation with Knox and Luke, or the clouds outside the window. Instead, my mind kept drifting to her and how she'd smile or make the simplest things feel important.

The weird thing was, she wasn't gone, not physically. But it was like I could sense that absence in a way I hadn't expected. I kept thinking about how she made everything feel a little more comfortable, a little more right. There was a stretch of time she was having a hushed conversation, and it made her feel a million miles away.

It was one of those things you don't realize until it's there, this sudden, quiet ache. I didn't expect it. But yeah, I missed her.

I couldn't get off the plane fast enough, and waited impatiently for her right outside the exit. As soon as I saw her, I retrieved her bag and placed my hand on the small of her back leading her towards the baggage area. It was a small touch, but contact with her was something I needed more than my next breath.

The bus ride to the resort was worse. We were shuttled in two separate vans, making the 45 minute ride feel like an eternity.

"I feel like we've been traveling for days," she whispers in my direction while we wait in line for our room.

I reach over and readjust the strap of her purse. It's only slightly twisted, but the adjustment allows me to make just enough contact with her to ensure she's here, within reach. Her breath hitches and, fuck, I love the way she reacts to my touch.

"Right!" I agree. "I could use a cold drink and a nap by the pool.

"That sounds amazing." She hums in approval.

The concierge approaches, interrupting this light moment between us, "Please, have a seat, my lady, and we will bring you some rum punch." A gentleman in a suit escorts us to a small loveseat not far from the counter.

"Your room will be ready in a few minutes. There are warm cookies in the jar in front of you."

He smiles and walks away.

"How in the world did everyone else get their rooms so fast?" she wonders aloud. The way she's sitting, rolling her fingers over the rim of the glass tells me everything I need to know. She needs to ground herself.

I brush my ankle against hers, "They're missing out on the punch. This is delicious." That small contact brings her eyes up so they meet mine.

"This might be the only thing I drink while I'm here," she adds after taking her first sip.

A few minutes later the gentleman comes back, "Your room is ready, and your bags have been delivered."

"Thank you," I hand him a tip, and follow him to our room.

Our room is just a few buildings over, tucked away in its own little corner of the resort. It's a short walk, but every step brings me closer to something more stunning. The moment we arrive, I can't help but pause and take it all in. The view is absolutely breathtaking.

From our balcony, you can see the entire stretch of beach, the soft sand glistening under the sun, and the water is a mesmerizing shade of turquoise that fades into deep blues as it stretches into the horizon. The gentle waves roll in lazily, crashing softly against the shore, creating a soothing soundtrack for everything around us.

The palm trees sway with the breeze, their long fronds rustling as if they're speaking in whispers. The whole scene feels like something out of a postcard, almost unreal.

The room is small, but it's got this cozy charm to it. There's barely enough space for the essentials. There is just a bed and a small table tucked against one wall. The bed, though, is comfortable, perfect for collapsing into after a long day of exploring the island. It's not the kind of room where you have much floor space to move around, but that's ok because everything you need is right within arm's reach. It's like being wrapped up in a calm cocoon.

The concierge excuses himself after giving us a quick rundown, and as he closes the door, April's voice fills the room.

"Um… I was banking on us having a couch one of us could sleep on, or enough floor space to make up a bed." The panic in her voice is clear.

"We can put pillows between us," I reassure her.

"Pillows will make me ho—" April spins around and her gasp makes me laugh. "What the hell is that?" She drags out her words for emphasis.

The window that looks straight into the shower is a bit unusual. It's not the kind of window you'd expect, it's actually a little creepy.

"I'm guessing so you can have a romantic view while you shower," I respond by putting my hands on her shoulders to calm her. "We can figure out how to hang a sheet or something."

She puts her hands over her eyes and mutters, "Cash, not only do we have to share a bed, we have to watch each other shower, this is a little too kinky for me."

"No, we *get* to, Tulip."

She arches a brow in confusion, "What?"

"Get to see each other shower," I correct her. "We don't have to, we get to." I wiggle my brows for effect.

She takes a deep inhale, and walks over to her bag. "I can't be in here right now, it feels like I'm suffocating."

She pulls a bathing suit out of the bag and makes her way into the bathroom to change. Should I break it to her that I can also see the mirror from here and it's offering me a first class view?

No. I'll let her figure that out herself. I don't want to freak her out even more.

Thank fuck the toilet is behind a door.

I decide to change out here so we can go to the pool as soon as she's done.

Minutes later, she emerges, and my heart stops. She is not what you would expect. Modest, yet stunning. She is wearing a flowery one piece and a long flowy over thingy with bouncy sleeves. She has her sunglasses on her head, a floppy hat in her hand, and sandals on her feet. She is breathtaking.

"Let me grab a clip for my hair, and we can go," she says softly, rustling through her bag until she pulls one out.

"That's an odd clip," I remark when the thing she pulls out looks nothing like I expected.

"It's flat so I can lay down in the sun and it won't hurt my head."

"That's cool," I offer, not really having anything insightful to say. "Want to grab some food? I'm starving."

"Sure. I'll also put some of our snacks in the bag since we didn't eat them on the plane."

She bends over to load the snacks in a pool bag she had in her suitcase, and I can't help but wish she wasn't hidden behind this colorful little robe thingy.

I glance down at her suitcase on the floor and stop in my tracks.

"Why hello, Marry Poppins."

"What?"

"How much is packed in that tiny little suitcase?"

She laughs. "Enough for all the days. Let's go."

We grabbed a quick bite and headed to the pool. Everyone else must be up in their rooms, because there is not a familiar face in sight.

I sit at the edge of the pool, my feet just barely skimming the surface of the water. The heat is still heavy, but the coolness of the pool is enough to make it bearable. Everything is calm, except for April. She's lying on her towel nearby, one hand tucked under her head, her hat tilted just enough that I can catch a glimpse of her eyes, and they carry so much stress.

"You know, you're awfully quiet. Isn't this the part where you hit me with some random, deep philosophical thoughts?"

She doesn't move, but I can see her lips twitching. "I didn't realize I was supposed to entertain you. You're not bored, are you?"

I grin, leaning back. "Not yet. But it's only a matter of time."

April finally turned her head, skepticism all over her expression. "Oh, really? Being in Jamaica isn't entertaining enough? What exactly is making you so bored? Me not talking enough? Or the fact that you've been staring at me for the past five minutes?"

I chuckle, pretending to look innocent. "I wasn't staring. I was just observing."

"Right," she says, a sarcastic edge creeping into her voice. "Observing what, exactly?"

"Just… trying to figure out if I'm the only one here who knows how to have fun." I give her a teasing look.

She tilts her head, her lips curling into a smile. "I'm just enjoying the quiet. Not everyone needs to be entertained like a little kid craving a pooltime competition."

I raise an eyebrow. "So you're telling me you're not going to challenge me to anything today? I'm kind of disappointed."

April shoots me a side eye, clearly amused. "Oh, don't worry. I'm sure you'll get your challenge… eventually."

The way she says it leaves me intrigued. "Eventually, huh? You're planning something, aren't you?"

She shrugs nonchalantly, her eyes glinting with that familiar spark. "You'll see."

I lean forward, my curiosity getting the better of me. "Come on, give me something to work with. What's the game plan here?"

She gives me a sly grin. "If you're so curious, why don't you just make me show you?"

Before I can react, she jumps up and dives into the pool with a splash. I barely have time to blink before she's gliding through the water, looking back over her shoulder at me, daring me to follow.

"Oh, it's on," I mutter under my breath as I dive in after her.

The chase is on, and I'm not about to let her get away with this silent game she's playing.

Every time I think I have her, she slips just out of reach, her laughter echoing through the water, daring me to try harder.

This isn't about getting her to talk or make a move, it's about melting that cold exterior she's been wearing with me.

"You're fast as shit, Tulip."

She stops and spins around. "You've already used that one? A few times now. Running out of witty things to call me?"

"You remind me of a tulip, you open up when you're in the right environment full of people or experiences you love, but you're more closed off and you kind of shut down when you don't want to deal with things."

She is assessing my assumption, and I can't tell how it's sitting with her, so I continue, case in point, "Like right now, you were having fun, and blossoming, but then the mood shifted and you're closing me out." I brush my hand across her shoulder and lean in, "But, I love that you're letting me see the brighter side a little bit more each day. I'll work for the privilege, Tulip."

You Make Me Feel Something...

"Girl I've been waitin' on this long hard day to get over,
so I can rest my head right here on your shoulder."

-Dierks Bentley

April

AFTER LEAVING THE POOL, Cash and I came back to the room to get ready, but he decided to go back down to the bar for a drink while I showered to give me some privacy.

Only when he came back up, I was still getting ready, and we had limited time before we were supposed to meet everyone for dinner. I told him I'd be busy doing my makeup in the floor length mirror so he could shower. He didn't seem to be as bothered by the lack of privacy the giant window offered.

I tried to concentrate on my makeup, but every time I looked in the mirror I got a glimpse of his rippled back, carved by hours of work in the gym. He is quite literally the most perfect specimen. When you add on the charm and intense attention he offers, I'm at a loss. How in the world is he still single?

My thoughts are interrupted by the sight of him coming out of the steamy bathroom in nothing but a towel. My head spins, and my vision slows, creating a movie-like montage of his movements in my mind. My heart is reliving the moment McSteamy emerged from the bathroom in Addison's hotel room, only this time it's beating a little faster, because the hot man in a towel is not on my TV, but right here in the flesh.

Now I'm hot. It came creeping in low and slow, curling through me like smoke. My pulse kicks up as my gaze drifts over him, and when the towel hits the floor, I realize, this time my body isn't betraying me in its normal way, the betrayal is a reaction to *him*.

Then he turns to grab his shorts out of his bag, holding said towel in front of his jewels, and I can't help but wish he'd drop it.

"You're drooling Tulip." His laughter startles me and I drop my mascara.

"You dropped your towel, who does that?" I try my hardest to fake an ounce of disgust in my voice, but it's no use. I liked it, and he knows it.

The vision of his towel hitting the floor swirled through my mind all night at dinner.

Now, laying in bed beside him with a giant stack of pillows between us, it's still all I see.

An unfamiliar warm sensation builds between my legs, the one I crave, but rarely get.

Only right now with his scent wrapped around me, and the room too quiet to pull my thoughts away, Blake and Ana's words come creeping in. What if they're right? What if I'm my own worst enemy and I'm the only thing keeping myself from apparent bliss?

I slowly reach down and snake my hand down beneath the blankets and lazily glide my fingers around my aching clit. It feels good, no doubt, but Cash is right there, so I reposition myself, turn towards the window, and try to lull myself to sleep.

The only problem, curiosity comes creeping back in, and after what seems like hours but is most likely minutes, I can't take it anymore. I have to try.

I sneak out of the bed and pad across the room to the bathroom. I leave the light off, not wanting to wake Cash, and decide to sit on the bench in the shower so I can watch out this creepy little window to make sure he doesn't wake, but as I start to lay lazy circles around my clit through my sleep shorts, I feel like a complete creeper.

If he wakes up to me touching myself while watching him through the shower window, it will be a scene right out of my nightmares.

I shift, trying to peer out of the window to make sure he's asleep, and that's when I realize the picture hanging on the wall next to the shower in the bathroom slides over the window.

"You've got to be fucking kidding me," I groan to myself.

Quietly, I slide the picture across the track, ensuring the window is covered. I leave the light off, and decide to get undressed and take a shower. The newfound privacy relaxes me, and if he wakes up, he'll just think I'm taking a shower now that his view inside is blocked.

Deciding I need to take the girls' advice and find what works for me, I grab the detachable shower head and let the rivulets of water work me into a shallow frenzy. Pressure ebbs and flows through my core and I start to move the wand around locating a few perfect positions.

I close my eyes and lean back on the wall, focusing on the sensation building between my legs, but the sensation of emptying my bladder takes over, and I jump out to go pee, only nothing really comes out. By the time I get back in, the sensation is gone.

"Why?" I groan. Starting all over again, I reposition the shower head. Only this time, nothing happens. The water feels like awkward pressure instead of a welcome sensation, and my head has already taken over, thinking of Cash waking up, me making too much noise. The moment is gone and I'm too frustrated to try again. Who knows how long I've been here, but to me, it's already been too long. I tried, and the idea that I confirmed my own suspicions about my body will make it easy to sleep. I dry myself off and make my way back to bed.

Cash

S HE SHIFTED BEHIND THE fortress of pillows she reluctantly stacked between us. She's rearranged them four times, and it makes me wonder why she put them there in the first place. The sliver of bed I had was not comfortable by any measure of the word, so I was only in a veiled fog of sleep. My back was to her, so I was facing the window to the shower when she entered it, sitting on the bench, peering to make sure I was still asleep as she rolled her fingers over her sleep shorts.

"Fuck," I whisper to myself.

I watch for a moment, not even a little sorry that she's unaware she has an audience. However, my heart sinks a little when she pulls the picture across the track blocking my view of the shower. Of course I noticed the picture before. No way in hell I was telling her about it.

There's a sizable gap between the picture and the wall due to the track, so I move my position, sitting up against the headboard. My new position offers me the slightest peek into the shower, but my view is obstructed by the blanket of darkness that fills the entire room. Every few seconds I would get a sliver of skin, she had undressed, but I couldn't tell what part of her body the skin covered.

Honestly, it doesn't matter. She's naked, touching herself in the shower, maybe because of me.

That thought sends my cock twitching in my shorts. I wiggle, sliding them down slightly, wrapping my hand around the base of my cock stroking it lightly at first. As my imagination goes wild with images of her pert tits dripping with water and her fingers rubbing between her legs, my speed increases. I bring my hand to my mouth, releasing a small amount of spit into my palm, imagining the wet sensation around my shaft is her mouth sucking me in. Normally I'd be imagining a pussy wrapped around my dick, but I want to save all images of that for the real thing.

I pump up and down imagining her blue eyes staring up at me, her lips wrapped around me, pulled taut. As I increase my pace, I see images of her eyes filling with tears as I push all the way into her mouth, and squeeze my hand around my dick as I imagine her throat constricting. The images keep flashing, until I feel a pull deep in my balls and I release hot spurts coming onto my stomach.

Damn, I want her so bad.

I quickly get out of bed and grab a few tissues from the table to clean myself and place them in the trash, climbing back in bed just before I hear the water turn off.

A few minutes later, she emerges from the bathroom, and I watch her cross the dark room, my eyes fixed on her, knowing she can't see mine. She seems… tense. The muscles in her shoulders are rigid, and she is whispering something under her breath that I can't make out. She is not at all in the shroud of post-orgasm bliss I'm living in.

Do orgasms make her angry?
Why is that thought hot as hell?

She is tossing and turning, and she seems way too in her head. I want to reach over and comfort her, but that would give me away, and I don't want to break down the small shreds of trust I've built with her, so I stay where I am, eyes closed.

Somewhere between her heavy agitated breaths and the sound of the waves outside, I fell into a deep sleep. When I awake, she's sitting up next to me in bed reading. The sun is shining, and I can hear people swimming outside.

"Morning, Tulip," I say in a sleep-coated breath.

"Good morning." She looks rested, and her face is stunning, void of makeup and her hair in a loose bun on top of her head.

"Why didn't you wake me?"

"You looked cozy, and I was comfortable, and wanted an excuse to read." Her smile's bright.

"Did you sleep ok? I heard you get in the shower in the middle of the night."

She stiffens next to me. "Yeah my legs were restless, and the hot water helps calm them." She coughs to hide her paranoia.

Yeah I bet your "legs" were real restless.

"Oh, there's a picture that covers the window, I left it closed so you could shower in privacy this morning," she adds.

"What time is it?" I ask, genuinely curious. We're supposed to have our pre-wedding day of fun, but she doesn't seem stressed like we're late.

"It's only 8. You have an hour and a half to go down to the lobby for golf, and I'll go down with you to meet the girls."

"Sounds good. I'll go get in the shower," I tell her as I rise from the bed, groggy from sleep.

I walk into the bathroom, but secretly wish I could climb back in bed and move the pillow fortress to hold her for just a few minutes before we have to face the rest of the world.

"Can I grab a hair tie before you get in the shower?" she asks, voice too casual, like she's not already halfway inside—like we're not already toeing the edge of something we never talk about.

She slips under my arm before I can shut the door, and suddenly we're tangled—too close, too familiar, in all the wrong ways. Her shoulder brushes my chest. Her skin finds mine. She's already holding her hair up, like she expected me to let her in.

"Sorr—" I start, but she says it too.

"Sorry."

She smiles.

And it hurts.

It's the kind of smile people give when they're pretending they don't want something more. One of the few she's ever given me that's real. And it just twists something deeper in my chest.

We freeze. My elbow pins her gently to the doorframe, like my body can't decide if it's trying to keep her in or push her out.

Her skin is warm against mine. Too warm. Too much. I don't breathe.

She looks at me—really looks—and says, soft and slow, "I should grab a hair tie so you can—"

"Get in the shower," I finish, because she can't.

"Yeah," she says. But she doesn't move.

Neither do I.

"Yeah," I echo, barely able to hear my own voice over the rush in my ears. I shift just slightly, enough that my arm is still braced above her on the frame, like if I moved any closer, I wouldn't be able to stop myself.

My lips are a breath from hers.

One breath.

That's all it would take.

To my surprise, she closes the distance even more. The change is barely noticeable, but I notice.

Then, like fate has a cruel sense of humor, her bathroom bag slips from the hook and crashes to the floor.

She startles, blinking like she forgot where she was. Who we are. What this *isn't*.

Frantic, she kneels to pick everything up, fingers trembling, shoving bottles and brushes into the bag like if she moves fast enough, it'll erase what almost happened.

"Let me—" I reach down to help, but she's already standing, already slipping past me with her eyes down and her mouth tight. The door clicks shut behind her before I can say another word.

As I turn and lean against the now closed door, I wonder, *What is she carrying that is so heavy she can't let herself trust me?*

Dancing, Drinking, and Definitely Not Missing You...

"I was a lone wolf, had my own back…"
-Lainey Wilson

April

I STARE AT MY phone, not knowing how to respond. I blink a few times, before Ana notices.

"You good?" she asks.

I don't respond, I just flip my phone around so she can see the texts.

"Shit, now that sounds like the guy Knox talks about." She smiles.

"I don't know what to say to him," I admit.

"Don't know what to say to who?" Blake asks as she walks up to us. She walked the guys to the shuttle taking them to the golf course and I'm sure her and Luke had a mushy goodbye. They can't seem to bear being apart.

I turn the phone to show her the messages as well.

"Wow, that's… nice." She seems as caught off guard as I do. "Wait, what do you mean you don't know what to say?"

"It's just a little unexpected," I try to explain, but they both look at me like I was sending him a hand-written thank you note by a carrier pigeon.

"Say thank you," Blake finally says, stating the obvious.

"Obviously." I roll my eyes, "But this is a sweet gesture, a thank you seems a little…" My words get tangled like piles of yarn in my brain. "Like it's not appreciative enough," I finally manage to get out.

"You can thank him properly later." Ana winks.

I roll my eyes at her, and wait a minute to gather myself before responding.

April: This is sweet, Cash. Thank you.

I type out the message as we make our way to breakfast and then check it a few times for a response, but nothing comes.

The girls and I get to the restaurant and luckily we sit at a table in the back corner away from most of the other guests, because Blake and Ana have been relentless since we took our seats, and our conversation is not one other guests would appreciate, even at an adult's only resort.

"You know it's time right?" Ana starts.

"Time for what?" I'm afraid to finish the question, and wish I could suck the words back in as they leave my mouth.

"To give him the goods," Blake teases. "He's trying. Really hard."

"No," I respond, and then quickly realize that would not be the response of a swooning girlfriend, "…better place than Jamaica, right?"

I sound like such an idiot.

"Why do you seem so weird about this?" Blake narrows her eyes not buying it.

"I'm not."

"April." She looks at me with a stern expression. She can see right through me. She knows me better than anyone.

"Are you afraid, you know, you won't finish?" Ana asks sheepishly.

I take the bait, this is the perfect decoy. "Well, it is inevitable." I sigh, knowing that part isn't a lie.

"Ok, walk us through it." Ana's voice is low and demanding.

I look at her with a puzzled expression.

She takes that as a cue to continue. "Walk us through what happens right before you, you know? You lose it."

"No, we can talk about this later. This week is about Blake. What do you want to do after breakfast?" I turn my attention to Blake, hoping to drop this.

"I want to help you get the big 'O', this feels like the perfect way to spend my wedding week, dirty talk, mimosas, and a massage to key me up. Perfect!"

"Ugh," I tease. "You have always been such a horndog, and he's my brother, remember?"

"Hearing it can't be worse than the day you accidentally walked in on us." She laughs.

"Don't remind me," I groan.

"That might not have been funny in the moment but it sure is now…" Ana adds. "Ok, now walk us through it."

"Well, when I'm actually in the mood, which is not often, it all feels good. I get worked up, there is a great build up, and then it gets too intense, and I have to pee. Every. Single. Time." I put a crisp emphasis on each word for impact.

"Ok. I'm not a doctor, but it sounds like you might actually be more sensitive down there than you think, and you're avoiding a potential mess," Blake suggests.

"I feel like I am not in control of my body."

"Oh, that's the best part of it. You just have to let go," Ana adds. "Just don't think about it."

"Maybe. I just can't—I feel so disconnected from my body." I sigh. I don't really know what else to say. "Let's go get more drinks, and hang by the pool until our massages. This is a little too much right now." I desperately want out of this conversation. There are too many layers to my inability to finish, and this is not the time to bring up my current condition.

The spa is absolutely gorgeous. Tucked behind tall wooden fences, it feels like a secret sanctuary. The air is rich with the calming scents of eucalyptus and coconut, blending into a warm, tropical embrace. Small, open huts, draped in natural wood and thatch, sit nestled among lush greenery. Soft lighting dances on the walls, while the distant sound of water trickling over stones adds to the tranquility. The air is warm but fresh, cool breezes whispering through the trees. Every detail invites you to unwind, offering a serene escape that touches every sense.

I settle under the warm blanket on the table, and instantly feel at ease.

Before the masseuse comes in, I take a quick selfie and shoot it off to Cash.

April: This spa is absolutely beautiful, and so relaxing. Thank you, again.

I reach over to the little stand next to the table and exchange my phone for the warm towel she instructed me to lay over my face, getting settled right before the masseuse knocks on the door.

As the warm oils glide over my skin, their soothing heat slowly melts away the tension in my muscles. The gentle pressure of the masseuse's hands works rhythmically, easing the tightness in my shoulders. But as I begin to sink into the peacefulness of the moment, my mind drifts, unexpectedly, to him. Cash. I smile softly to myself, thinking about the way he thoughtfully picked snacks for me, how his touch felt like comfort and chaos all at once when I fell asleep on his shoulder during the flight.

I think about the little things I've come to enjoy with him, the banter, the way we effortlessly tease back and forth, his knack for picking the perfect thing to say in every situation. How his presence seemed to warm every room. The plethora of nicknames he uses when he talks to me, the way he settled on Tulip. I never realized how much I would love having a nickname. Right now he feels a million miles away, and somehow closer than anyone ever has. It's funny how a person can start to fill the spaces in your life without you even noticing it.

I think back to Blake talking about the couples' massage her and Luke booked, and it makes me wish he was here to enjoy this with me. I bet his body takes a beating while training, and this would be such a needed relief.

Shit… I'm missing him.

A sharp wave of panic hits, and I feel the walls closing in. What is wrong with me? Why can't I just let go and give myself what I clearly want?

I hear the calm rhythm of the ocean waves around me, echoing through the speakers that fill the room—attempting to make it appear like we are not on the other side of the resort from the beach—and it could not be more opposite of the tidal wave raging inside me.

If he were here, he'd notice my tension. I know he would, and he would instantly know how to make it better. With nothing more than a brush of our fingertips laying next to each other.

I imagine it, and instinctively take a deep breath.

I take another, and another, trying to steady my heart. This is different. He is different.

Different than I believed.

Different can be good. Right?

I COORDINATED MASSAGES FOR the girls for several reasons.

One, I apologized to Blake for the misunderstanding between us, but I want to make sure she knows exactly how sorry I am. Plus, she deserves to be pampered during her wedding weekend.

Two, my girl. She deserves the world, every bit of beauty and wonder it has to offer her, and I will stop at nothing to show her I'm the man who can give it to her. I want to break through the walls around her heart, gently but surely, until she sees that I'm not just here for a moment, but for all of it.

I get the impression that she's never really been in a good relationship. At first she was distant because she thought I was a dick, but her distance has shifted. It's resemblant of someone who has been hurt, or had love fall flat.

My mission is to help her see what a relationship could be like.

Should be like.

Some would say I'm falling hard, but the truth is, I'm already gone.

"Where the hell is the beer cart?" Keith, one of Luke's friends asks. "I'm not wandering around in this heat without a drink."

"Don't play much golf?" Luke jokes.

"Nope, don't really plan on changing that today, either." He laughs. "I have a date with some Red Stripe."

"I thought sassy brunettes were more your type," Ty cuts in. "Or is Isa over your ass already?"

"You fucking wish," Keith says sarcastically.

"Fuck. I changed my mind," Luke groans. "You two fuckers are going by yourselves. I'm going with Cash and Knox." He laughs as he rolls his hand over his face and then jumps on the back of our cart.

When we get to the first tee box I step up to the tee, gripping the club like I actually know what I'm doing. Golf has never been my thing, and swinging a baseball bat and a golf club are not the same.

The wind's blowing just enough to be annoying, and I'm trying to ignore the fact that Knox and Luke are watching me like I'm about to make or break the entire round.

Knox, the fucker that he is, is standing a few feet away, already critiquing my stance. Is he a golfer? No. But now that he trains athletes, apparently he thinks he can train me too.

"You're not rotating enough through the hips," he says like I'm about to screw up a highlight reel for a recruiter for the PGA. "You gotta—"

"Knox, I'm just trying to hit the fucking ball," I interrupt. "It will be really fucking embarrassing if I can't even make contact, and I need every ounce of focus I can muster. So, please, shut the fuck up."

He looks at me like I just said I was going to kick the ball instead of swing it. "You need to—"

"Knox, let it go," Luke chimes in from behind, popping a beer. "Let him have his moment. Besides, I'm pretty sure 'rotating through the hips' is some sort of… baseball thing, not a golf thing."

Knox rolls his eyes.

I nod at Luke, thankful for the distraction, and take a deep breath.

I swing.

The ball goes straight… but not the way I wanted. It flies *directly* into the rough to the right of the green.

"Fuck," I say, setting up a new tee. "I'll just hit a new ball, I'm not climbing though that shit."

Knox, standing near the cart now, bursts out laughing.

I shoot him a look. "Shut up, Knox. This is a warmup."

"Just like when we played college ball together, you can't stand to lose," he mocks. "Watch." He walks over, tosses my ball at me to catch and sets up his shot.

This motherfucker. His ball goes straight up the fairway at least 300 yards.

"Knox, man," my voice is sheer disbelief. Last time we played he sucked, "When was the last time you played golf? You used to hit the ball like you were swinging a bag of dicks."

"When you enter into a corporate space trying to attract sponsors, you learn to golf. The course is where all my deals are made." He staggers off with the cockiest fucking grin.

When Knox stepped in to show me how to do it, I lost the chance to hit another ball, so now I'm still trying to locate the fucking thing in the rough, and every time I hear any ounce of movement my stomach drops.

If a fucking snake comes at me, I'm out.

It's like looking for a needle in a haystack, but I'm committed. I will find the motherfucker.

"Found it!" I call out, determined to get all the shit out of my way as I chop at the tall grass with my club.

"Just take a drop," Knox yells.

"Fuck off."

I swing.

The ball… goes straight into the water.

"I can't seem to hit the target today, on the course or with April," I mutter.

I'm getting a fucking beer.

"Alright, new rule," I say, tossing my club down. "No more serious talk. From now on, we're just *hitting* shit."

Luke raises an eyebrow. "Hitting shit?"

I grin. "Yeah, pick the target."

"Isn't the pin the target?" Knox asks.

"Not anymore. Bench," I call out, lining up my shot for the bench. "If I hit it, next round's on one of you assholes. If I miss it, I'll pay," I add.

"You're going to be broke as fuck by the time we finish the front nine." Knox laughs, clearly not even questioning my logic anymore.

"We're playing my game now," I say swinging the club, and what do you know, I fucking hit it. The ball ricochets off the bench and I turn around with a huge grin.

Fucking around. My kind of game.

"Who's paying, assholes?"

"Ok, Cash, your way of playing golf is way more entertaining than the traditional way," Luke laughs.

I go to respond, but get pulled into a haze of lust as my phone buzzes and I come face to face with the most captivating picture of April on my screen.

Her hair is thrown up in a messy bun piled on top of her head. Her face is completely void of makeup, and is illuminated by the soft glow of a nearby light in what appears to be a dark room. She is glowing, and looks completely relaxed. Her smile is slightly crooked propped up on her hand as the other is clearly holding her phone to take the picture.

I instantly make it my screen saver. I want this to be the first thing I see every time I take a call, check an email, mindlessly scroll my socials, or simply just admire it by clicking the button on my phone when I'm not with her.

This picture of her is the purest form of perfection encapsulated in a single image. This is the face I've been looking for my entire life.

If she asked me to quit everything and move to some godforsaken beach hut, I'd start packing.

The Jig Is Up

"I wanna breathe you in…"

-Dierks Bentley

April

THE GIRLS AND I went to the little karaoke bar on the resort, and were singing our lungs out when I saw the guys walk by outside. Karaoke is set up in a small lounge attached to a bar, complete with a large sectional around the perimeter of the room facing a giant screen where the words project. Behind the plush couch are floor to ceiling windows. That's where Cash is, on the other side of the glass, when I spin around, belting 'Pink Pony Club'.

For the most part, our time here has been pretty chill, a few people here and there have recognized Cash, and if there have been more, we wouldn't know it. Everyone's been very respectful of his privacy.

The group of girls who've flocked him outside the bar, not so much. I'm not even sure if they know who he is, as much as just think he's gorgeous. Either way, the tall blonde in the middle wants him. Bad. They follow the guys into the bar attached to the lounge we're in, and the second they enter, all of the air seems to leave my lungs. My lungs constrict, my hands turn clammy, and my heart's pounding out of my chest. But the sensation, jealousy, only lasts a few seconds, because the second he sees me the rest of the room, including the one trying her darndest to put her tits in his face, disappears.

His eyes lock on mine and he stares for a moment before licking his lips and summoning me to him with a come hither motion of his finger. It's fucking hot. I move towards him, but don't have to move far before he's on me, pulling me into a deep kiss.

I hesitate for a moment, before melting into it, knowing this is natural, we're a couple, this is what couples do. They kiss.

I lose track of the blonde he was talking to, he clearly wasn't interested so I shouldn't be either.

His lips are velvet on mine, smooth and warm. He slowly wraps his hand around the nape of my neck, deepening the kiss and my insides become an inferno. His tongue dances lazily across mine, the rhythm natural and familiar. He kisses me as if he'd been away for months.

Missing me.

Longing for me.

Only had eyes for me.

"That was quite the show," I pant. "Sorry you had to play the part instead of taking her back to your bed."

"The only one I want in my bed, Tulip, is you. You look good enough to eat."

His words hang in the air, dense and consuming.

He was drunk from a day of golf, dinner on the catamaran with the guys, and whatever shenanigans they'd been up to all night. That didn't matter though, they're still on repeat in my head as I lay next to him in bed. He left insinuation heavy in the air, if I wanted him, I could have him.

Everyone called it a night shortly after our heated makeout session. After all, the wedding is tomorrow, and we have to be in tip-top shape for the festivities.

Cash is asleep and has been since he hit the bed a few hours ago.

The damn pillows between us are making me hot, so I throw them on the floor now that he's asleep.

He lightly snores when I move the last pillow, but doesn't wake. Clearly he's in a deep slumber. Me? I'm still thinking about that kiss, staring into the dark abyss surrounding me. While this time feels different, insomnia is nothing new for me, but after hours laying in the dark, wondering what it would be like to actually let go and have him, my eyes succumb to the weight, and I drift into a deep sleep.

"Oh, please. Don't stop," I pant as he lazily rubs his fingers over my clit.

The motions are soft and delicate, almost featherlike, causing my insides to ache.

"Hummmm," he moans in my ear. The sound spurs a desire deep inside me. A desire to see him come undone. I fumble with the waistband of his shorts, wigging my hand beneath the fabric. When I reach the tip of his cock—thick, heavy, already slick with anticipation—my eyes shoot open.

It's huge.

I bring my hand to my mouth and drop a small bead of spit into my palm and return it to his thick erection behind me. Every motion I make feels heavy, coated in sleep, as I begin moving up and down his length and he growls a low mumble of words I can't make out.

Just then he dips his fingers, sliding two inside me and begins to massage my clit, or maybe the spot just beneath my lips. It feels like he is pulling me to his chest. The sensation feels distant, and everywhere consuming me all at once. I am having a hard time pinpointing where his hands are, where my hands are... we're spooning, I think.

"Wake up," I tell myself as I try to fight the sleepy haze I'm in. I can't have a sex dream about him, next to him.

My brain is foggy and my thoughts are jumbled as I shimmy out of my panties and then softly free him the rest of the way from his briefs. I lead the head of his dick to my opening and when he pushes inside, it takes me a second to adjust.

The full sensation, the slight sting from my slick pussy stretching as it tries to make room for him pulls me a little farther out of my sleep-coated haze, but as much as I know I need to, I'm not ready to leave this dream yet.

I pull him closer to me and adjust to make room for him to slide a little farther inside me. As his erection massages the edge of my cervix something happens.

My breath quickens.

I break out in sweat.

My walls tighten.

My body starts shaking.

The air is thick and warm.

"Cash, please don't stop!" I yell, pulling my pillow over my face as more quakes run through me.

That's when I realized this isn't a dream at all…just a sleepy, haze-filled fantasy playing out in that strange mental space right before you fully wake up.

"Shit." He stills behind me for a blink. "April." His voice is low gravely, and a guttural moan leaves his mouth as he continues pumping inside me.

This is not a dream, I reiterate to myself.

He is inside me.

I actually guided him inside me, not just in my dream, and it feels so goddamn good.

"Fuck, I'm going to come," is all he says as he shimmies out from behind me and groans, a small spurt of come settling on my ass.

Slipping fully out of the haze, I sit up to find him buried in the sheets below the waist, with them crumpled around his dick as he breaks out in goosebumps and his body convulses.

My hands cover my face, I can't catch my breath.

"Oh my god. Oh, shit. Cash. Oh my god. I just…" I panic and my breath quickens. "I just. I was asleep and… I'm sorry."

He moves closer to me and drapes his hand over my shoulder. "Breathe. It's… Fuck, Tulip. Don't be sorry. You just fulfilled every man's fantasy of waking up deep inside a hot chick. You felt incredible. That was the best way I can imagine waking up."

"I started that didn't I?" I wince.

"Beats me. I thought I was dreaming until you screamed my name. You scared the shit out of me." He chuckles.

"I'm sorry. I thought *I* was dreaming," I try to explain.

"I'm only sorry I wasn't fully awake." His smile is genuine and soft.

I'm mortified. Heat burns up my neck to my face like a wildfire. My stomach twists into knots as a small strangled sound leaves my mouth. But the embarrassment quickly shifts to disappointment.

"April. It's ok. It happens. I think. I'm sure this happens to couples all the time. Pent up energy and sexy dreams turning to reality in a sleep-filled fog."

"I don't really remember it." I shake my head. "No, no, no, no, no."

"We were sleeping. We can pretend it didn't happen," he tries to reassure me.

"The first time, and it slipped away, and I don't even remember it." My head is still buried in my hands as I turn to hang my feet off the edge of the bed.

"We can do it again?" It's a question, I think. Confusion laces his voice.

I break out in laughter, because who does this? Who initiates sex because they think they're dreaming, but in reality they're just horny?

"Cash," I cringe, not believing I'm going to divulge this to him, "I'm not freaking out because we had sex, that was my first orgasm. I think. And I missed it. I was half asleep, and it happened before I could actually process it."

He just stares at me for a second. He's not even blinking. It feels like 10 minutes go by, but it's more likely ten seconds before he speaks. "You *think*?"

I roll my eyes. "Why do you always pull out the most miniscule part of what I say to focus on?"

"Miniscule?" he huffs. "We just had sex, and you *think* you had your first orgasm… meaning you're not sure."

"This isn't about you, Cash. I don't know because I've never had one."

"Not even alone?"

"Cash. Listen to me. I've. Never. Had. One. Before."

The sting sinks in. The disappointment in the realization that I *think* it really is all it's cracked up to be, but I still can't be 100% sure. Why is never experiencing true pleasure a decision my body gets to make without me?

Cash

I HEAR HER WORDS, but I'm having a hard time catching up. I was sleeping. Dreaming about her. Then the most incredible sensation fell over me. Slick warmth spread across me leaving a lingering tingle in its wake. It wasn't just heat, it was liquid fire, delicate, smooth, like a whispered secret as it spread. I was bare inside her. I've never been bare before, and that was the best feeling to wake up to.

When she screamed my name and I realized what was happening, I didn't know what to do, and before I knew it, I was a goner. Enjoying it until I realized there was nothing between us. I should have pulled out sooner, but the second I felt her, all logic left the room. My release was already there, I hurried out of her just in time to spill into the sheets. It was the best feeling in the world, and I almost missed it, so I understand how she's feeling right now. But fuck, I can't let that be her first and only experience with a climax.

If I were any other guy, my ego wouldn't fit in this room right now. I'm the first one to give her an O. Only instead I'm disappointed for her. I'm broken as I stare into her blue eyes, deep and empty.

She missed it.

Fuck that!

I should be delicate. I should ease her in, but my need to rectify this for her is too strong.

I get up from my side of the bed and stalk towards her side. She doesn't realize it at first, I'm certain by the shock in her eyes as I pull her legs hard, causing her shoulders to fall back on the mattress.

Her protests are weak and empty as I settle between her legs. They fall away the second my tongue grazes her clit.

"Ca— Cash." Her voice shakes as I lay soft strokes over her swollen flesh.

I lick, tug her clit between my lips, working her into a frenzy. She is pulling my hair, and gripping my head between her thighs as she pants out my name.

Then she shifts, readjusting her position.

Her grip on my hair loosens.

She groans in frustration, and sits up pulling herself away from me.

"What just happened?" I ask her, confused.

"The same thing that always happens. I lost it."

I stand, my erection bobbing as I make my way to the closet. I never bothered putting my boxers back on, and we're way past me giving a shit if she sees what she does to me.

I move back to the bed, my tie, headphones, and a cold beer bottle from the fridge in hand. She crooks her head to the side, clearly trying to decipher what I have planned. But I'm done talking. I have all the information I need. Now it's time to listen and learn, both of us. Not just me.

I start an instrumental playlist on my phone and place the headphones over her ears. She questions me with a skeptical look, but goes with it.

When I place the tie over her eyes, it's a different story.

"Cash," she protests, but just as before, it's weak and short lived.

She allows me to fasten it as I lay soft kisses over her cheeks, neck, and collarbone.

I gently place one hand behind her head and the other just behind her left knee and guide her to lay on the pillows.

I pull one side of the headphones far enough away that she can hear me.

"Just relax, baby. I've got you. The only thing I want you to focus on is how I make you feel."

She responds with a deep shuddering breath, and nods her approval.

That's all I need. That tiny acknowledgment; she's ok with this, she trusts me, and is ready for me to worship her.

I take a second, just a few blinks to take her in. She's sprawled out on the bed in front of me. Naked from the waist down. Blindfolded, headphones on, breathing heavy enough that if these were not the circumstances, I'd be worried about her heart rate. She's confident though, she's not shying away from my gaze on her, or my touch. She wants this. She wants to know how it feels. I saw the disappointment in her eyes.

My kisses start soft and slow at her jawline. I move them just to the edge of her lips, and when she turns and leans into my touch, I take her lips in mine, and consume her taste.

While my lips are on hers and she is lost in the kiss, I lightly snake my hand under her shirt. She isn't wearing a bra, and her nipple is hard, pushing against the pads of my fingers as I roll it between them. She arches her back and moans. The noise is loud and full. I can tell she's unaware of her volume.

Perfect.

There is something standing in the way of chasing her release.

Maybe she's afraid to be too loud. Maybe she's afraid of the sensation, maybe she doesn't know what she likes.

She could be stuck in her own head. Whatever it is, she's getting past it tonight.

I glance at the clock. 1:52. We have hours to uncover the reason. She doesn't have to be in the bridal suit until 10:00, and if it takes every second until then to unlock her deepest desires, so be it. It will be the best reason for exhaustion in the world.

I lightly pepper kisses down her body, leaving little goosebumps in my path.

I push up her shirt so I can get a glimpse of her tits. They've fallen to her sides slightly, and I can't for the life of me understand why that makes women self conscious. They always try to perk them back up with their arms. Something she's not doing, which tells me she's not overthinking her appearance, so I know that's not what's stopping her.

Her body is perfect, petite. From her breasts, to her thighs, to her tiny little toes painted pink. I raise her foot and place a soft kiss on the pad of her foot. She smiles, and the sight takes the air from my chest. I work my way up her leg, kissing and licking my way to her perfect pussy, decorated with a small patch of hair and dripping wet.

She's aroused, so that's also not it. I slide a finger inside, watching as the tip of my finger disappears. I twist it and move, coating myself in her. I dip a second finger inside watching them disappear. Fuck.

She moans, the noises intensifying with each stroke.

Her breath quickens, and pink blotches start to cover her chest.

She is so close.

I take my other hand and pick up the bottle of beer, crested with frost. It was sitting near the freezer compartment, so it's crisp and cold.

I hold the neck of the bottle in my grip and slide my fingers out of her wet cunt, watching her drip as I use them to slide her open. When the cold glass of the bottle rolls over her clit, she writhes, screaming my name.

"Fuck, Cash!"

I smile. She can't see me, but I can see every inch of her. Her nipples pebble from the cold contact, and she wiggles into the cool feel of the bottle against her skin. I bend down and replace the cooling sensation with the warmth of my mouth.

"Oh shit!" her voice echoes through the room.

I plunge my fingers inside her, and feel her walls begin to tighten, so I add a third to fill her up. It's tight and warm.

Then I see it. Shifts her position, moving away from the feeling. It's subtle, but she shifts her hips just enough that the spot I was hitting moves just out of reach.

She's afraid to come.

I place the bottle on the nightstand and use that hand to pull her towards me, and straddle her legs, pinning them beneath me.

I start pumping my fingers in and out of her. I take my other hand and apply the tiniest amount of pressure to her stomach, just above her pelvic bone.

She moans loudly and rips the tie off her face.

"Cash. It's… oh my god." Her eyes roll back in her head. "It's too much."

I watch her come undone right before me. I don't stop. She doesn't ask me to. I would if she did. Instead she lays her head back down and places a pillow over her face.

I apply a little more pressure and increase my speed and she loses it. Soaking my hand, the sheets, my tie that landed between her legs. She is coated in sweat, her hair is plastered to her face, little curls peeking out on the side of her neck.

"Shit, I'm sorry." Her hands cover her face. " Why do I keep embarrassing myself with you?"

"April," I pull her hands down and make eye contact with her before I continue, "All you are doing is making my head big. Do you know how hard it is to get that kind of reaction out of women? How good it feels to know I made you feel that fucking good?"

"You're just saying that." Her voice cracks slightly.

"You want to bet?" I pick up my phone, open my social media app and it only takes me a few seconds and a quick search to find video after video of guys talking about how to make women squirt and why guys find it sexy as hell.

I play them for her until her shoulders relax and she bats my phone away laughing. "Ok you made your point."

She moves to get off the bed and winces, "We need new sheets."

"I'll call the front desk."

Her eyes shoot in my direction, "Cash, that is so embarrassing."

"I'll tell them we spilled something."

"Right, yeah. That's a good cover. I'm getting in the shower, I'm a mess."

I watch her walk away.

She is a fucking mess.

My beautiful fucking mess.

Better Than the Last Time

"Let me run my fingers down your back"

- Luke Bryan

April

WHEN BLAKE ASKED ANA and I to both be her maids of honor, I was honestly a little offended. We have been friends for years. We have history. But I've come to realize they do too.

Blake was there when I got my first period… way later than all my friends. We graduated together. Went to parties together. I was there for her, my family was there for her when hers disappeared. We have years of memories, and heartbreak.

They do too. They lived together, worked together, Blake was there when Ana clung to life. She stood by Ana's side when she found out she was pregnant, gave birth, and got married.

We equally have history, threads that hold us together, unbreakable no matter the storm. I was late to the realization, but Blake has needed us both, and been here for us both in different ways.

We didn't pick out bridesmaids dresses, and Blake is not in a fluffy white dress. It's not her style. She's a vision.

One I know my brother is equally expecting, and not prepared for. She is in a deep champagne dress with a sultry twist. There is a sexy thigh-high slit, delicate lace along a plunging neckline, and barely there straps that criss-cross her open back. Instead of a veil, she wears a vintage gold hairpin with tiny black diamonds that match her ring, which tucks her hair in soft loose waves. To complete the outfit are ivory snakeskin ankle boots, despite the beach setting.

Her bouquet almost steals the show. It's wild and untamed, with thistle, dried pampas, and black calla lilies, wrapped in leather cord.

Because Blake doesn't do matchy matchy and doesn't believe that love comes in one shade, Ana and I had zero guidance for our attire.

No color scheme.

No preferred fabrics or jewelry.

She showed us a picture of her dress that she had handmade by Bella from the lingerie parlor back home, and said, *"Complement it."*

Ana is in a bohemian style bronze jumper. It has a delicate lace back that complements the lace on Blake's front. It has an empire waist and is paired with a set of gold sandals. Her hair is pulled in an elegant ponytail accented by a dried floral clip.

I opted for a muted coral, one-shoulder dress with a maxi slit. My hair is down, in its natural curl pattern and my rose gold wedges peek out perfectly.

Blake made our bouquets. Simple and clean. Palm leaves draped in linen. Literally nothing matches, yet matches perfectly.

"Look at us," Blake says, turning towards the large floor-length mirror in the corner. "This is exactly what I imagined."

"I'm glad, B." I offer her a warm hug and relish in an onslaught of emotion overtaking me.

"Luke is going to lose it when he sees you," Ana chimes in.

"Oh, B, you look stunning," my mom says as she enters the room. "It's time."

Blake takes in a long breath and moves towards the door. Ana and I silently follow.

The ceremony location is breathtaking. We are up on a balcony just one floor above the beach. The tall glass wall behind the altar offers a perfect view of the ocean in the background. I was curious why Blake opted to come all the way to Jamaica and not have the ceremony on the beach, until this very moment. This offers all the beauty and ambiance of a beach wedding without the sand and wind.

In true Luke and Blake fashion, everything is simple, untraditional. As Ana and I walk side by side, my eyes instantly lock with my brother, standing on his own at the altar. While Blake has Ana and I by her side, Luke has a small, open-locket pin over his heart with DJ's picture on it, his friend who passed years ago. Luke said he was the only best man he needed, and seeing the pin now warms my heart.

Blake and Luke opted not to have chairs, but instead, have the few guests join them in a crescent near the altar, so naturally the next place my eyes land is on Cash, turned, like the other guests, watching us walk towards them.

His stare is fierce, the blue matching the ocean behind him. His gaze never leaves me.

Not when I make my way to the front opposite my brother.

Not when the doors open and Blake comes into view.

Everyone else turns to Blake, but his eyes stay intently on me.

I should be watching Blake walk toward Luke. Instead, I can't stop thinking about the way Cash looks at me. Like I'm the one in white. Like we're the ones about to say forever.

I force myself to shift my gaze to my best friend—strong, independent, and breathtaking.

I asked her this morning why she wasn't having someone walk her down the aisle, and her response was the most Blake thing I've ever heard her say.

"No one's giving me away. I never belonged to anyone but myself. I didn't grow up waiting for a hand to hold or a name to change." She smiled. "I'm not passing from one life to another, Ap. I'm not letting go of who I was. I'm just choosing who I want to become, and I want to become his partner for the rest of my life."

The ceremony was short. They exchanged vows provided by the officiant, and it was over, minutes after it started.

Intimate.

Simple.

Cash

L IGHT PINK... OR ORANGE, whatever it is, it's my new favorite color.

She's flawless, undone. Her hair is in messy little curls from the humidity that she's had a hard time taming. Her makeup is barely there, but her lips are still painted that pretty little pink. Her skin is kissed by the sun, and the darker she gets, the more freckles appear.

I want to count them. Trace them. They're the subtle little road map of my new favorite adventure. Her.

I couldn't take my eyes off her for the three minute entirety of the ceremony, and had it lasted any longer, I would not have.

"Dance with me, Tulip," I whisper in her ear as I hand her a drink. Rum punch. She wasn't lying when she said it was all she would drink.

"There's no dance floor, Cash."

"I don't care. It's a wedding and I love slow dancing."

"Yes. I know." Her voice turns sharp. "And I know what it leads to."

"Tulip, Look at me." I bend down and crane my neck so our eyes meet. "I have no expectations of you. I just want to get to know you. Be close to you. Dance with you."

"Right." She rolls her eyes.

"April, why are you so intent on me being this egotistical version of me you've made up in your head?"

"I'm not."

"Really? Are you sure about that, because from where I'm standing you look a lot like someone trying so hard to pull away, when all I want is for you to let me in."

Her silence is infuriating.

"This time is already better than the last time I was on a dance floor, because I'm standing here with you."

Her expression doesn't change, but her eyes meet mine now.

I pull her close to me and start swaying to the music. "Baby, last night, I couldn't sleep. Like a thief in the night, stealing every second I could to study every tiny freckle on your nose. There is so damn much I don't know about you that it consumes me. I was awake all night because I don't know your middle name, Tulip. I don't know what flavor pancakes are your favorite, if you've ever been to a major league game, your favorite flower, your biggest dreams, fears, what exactly turns you on or even what turns you off."

This feels like a big confession for a makeshift dance floor, but I don't actually give a shit. "And in the middle of the night, for some damn reason, there was nothing I wanted to know more than those things. I mean, fuck."

I lean in closer so my words are a whisper on her skin. "I love seeing what you look like all messy in the morning after a night of sleep, and how much you love a warm cup of coffee. I even love your love for baked goods, but I still want to know what kinds of things make you laugh when you're crying. I want to know every little thing, baby, the good, the bad, and even the ugly."

Without a word she grabs me by the hand and leads me down the stairs to the beach and sits across from me on a chair instead of next to me.

"Cash, we literally live on opposite sides of the country."

"That's a bullshit excuse and you know it. Let. Me. In," I plead with a lump in my throat.

She takes a long breath before a single tear rolls down her cheek.

Her eyes are still closed when she starts, her voice quiet and strained. "I didn't even get to try. That's the part that guts me. I never got to want it before it was taken away."

The tears become heavier, but her voice is still steady. Strained, yet steady. "My body… just quit. Like it made a decision I didn't get to be a part of. I have to take hormones just to feel like myself. Most times it works, but sometimes it doesn't. I'm tired of pretending like I'm fine when I feel like a stranger in my own skin."

I wait for her to continue, moving beside her and pulling her into me. I feel her tears hit my hand and it shatters something inside me. On the outside I'm calm and collected, tapping into the part of my brain that turns emotion off during an intense game. On the inside though, I'm a mess. My heart feels like it's pulling at my skin, wanting to break free and replace her broken one with mine.

"Is it life threatening?" It's the only thing that comes to mind, I can't lose her. I just got her.

A soft chuckle leaves her lips. "No, I'm at increased risk for a few things that are mitigated by medication, so it shouldn't be a thing. Worst case scenario, my life expectancy is two years shorter."

"Shit, cheeseburgers will do that to you."

She laughs a loud genuine laugh. The first one I've been privileged to hear, and it is beautiful. Loud, full, echoing in the night.

"Jokes," I say aloud.

"What?" she asks as she wipes her tears.

"Jokes make you laugh when you cry."

She leans in and kisses me. It's soft, barely a whisper across my lips. As soon as she pulls away, I slide my tongue across my lips to taste her… Cherry.

"It's kind of fucked up, you know?"

She tilts her head with curiosity.

"That I can't decide which tastes better. The salty sweetness of your pussy or the cherry on your lips."

There's that laugh again. I'm addicted to the sound.

"Susannah."

"Humm." I look at her in question.

"My middle name." She laughs again and it feels like it fills the entire sky. "You want to hear the weird part?"

"Of course, I love the weird parts."

"Don't make this dirty." She swats at me. "Most women get cravings for specific foods during pregnancy. When my mom was pregnant with Luke all she wanted was chocolate milk. But with me, her sense of smell was off the charts, and all she wanted was to smell her favorite flower, so when I was born, she searched and searched for a name with the flower as its meaning."

"Yeah?" I ask not knowing the point of this when she could be kissing me again.

"Yeah, it means tulip."

My lips are on hers. And this time, she opens for me. In more ways than one, and as my tongue glides against her lips, the taste of cherry enters my senses. It's rough and intense, and full of promise of what's to come.

"Wait, are you fucking with me?" I ask through a ragged breath.

"Yes," she laughs.

"Really?" I pull back.

"Yes," her laugh gets louder. "I had to. I'm sorry. I couldn't help myself."

She pulls me into a kiss, and this time she lets a little moan escape.

"You're an asshole, Tulip," I joke. A little annoyed, but loving how much lighter she is.

"Jokes, remember. Jokes make me laugh when I'm crying."

"Was any of that shit true?"

"Yes, all of it. Except the meaning. It means lily."

I pull her close and kiss the side of her head, "Let's get back to the wedding, Tulip."

She's the Sun

"It's been one of those days I don't wanna do twice"
- Gabby Barrett

April

I KNOW SCREWING WITH him was mean, he was being so genuine and romantic, but when things got too heavy, I did the only thing I know how… got the fuck out of it.

I'm a lot. I know I'm a lot and I am awkward, loud, and rarely serious. I'm pretty much the exact opposite of who I've been with Cash, so I had to give him a little glimpse into who I really am, before he gets too attached to this version of me he thinks he knows.

"Are you ready, Tulip?"

His words cut through the silence like a siren on a quiet night.

"Yeah." I smile.

"Where are we going again?"

"Is this how it would be with you?" I ask with a laugh, "You never knowing the plans and relying on me to tell you where you need to be?"

"Probably, I'm a terrible planner. Spontaneous, I do well. Planning not so much."

I roll my eyes, "We're going shallow water snorkeling."

"What the hell is shallow water snorkeling?"

"Well, I think it's pretty self explanatory, but it's just off the shore by a reef not too far from here."

"Look at all of the fish. There are so many."

"We are in the ocean," Cash laughs.

"You know what I mean. I wasn't expecting there to be so many this close to shore."

"Why is Ana hanging out on the shore?"

I giggle at his observation. "She is terrified of the ocean. She will only go ankle deep. She's worried she'll get swept away."

He just chuckles and goes back to looking at the fish, but while he's face down in the water, admiring the fish swimming around us, he intertwines his pinkie with mine. It's a small touch, just enough to make sure I'm still there. My pulse quickens at the interaction.

Man, he's good at this fake dating thing.

"Which one is your favorite?" he asks me the next time he pops out of the water.

"I really like the little brown ones he told us about, the ones that look like rocks."

"The rockfish? All of these colorful fish swimming by us, and the rockfish are your favorite?" He nudges my shoulder playfully.

"Sometimes beauty isn't obvious from the outside, Cash. Do you know how much strength and courage it takes to be out in the wide open, concealing yourself from the world so it can't hurt you? That's beauty." At least that's what I tell myself.

"Yeah, but the reef is right there, and can protect them. If they just move a little, they could have all the love and protection they want." His smile is so genuine, and we both know we aren't talking about the fish anymore, so I swallow the lump in my throat and try not to run or joke this time.

"Cash, sometimes looking for shelter doesn't solve the problem. Maybe they're concealing themselves until they learn how to truly tap into all the strength they have."

He stops talking about the fish and places a kiss on my forehead. "You seem pretty strong to me already, Tulip."

And then he swims away. The perfect man, trying to be my shelter from the storm brewing inside me, swims away and all I can bring myself to do is watch him.

"Let's take a selfie with the ocean behind us!" Blake suggests as we plop down on the beach chairs next to Ana, leaving the guys to hang out on the boat.

"What are you two doing over here? You're supposed to be enjoying all the fish." Ana's voice is bright and bubbly as she peeks over her Kindle.

"We did, and now we want to have a drink and relax before we head back." I stood from the chair, handed her a drink from the boat, and pulled her to her feet.

We pose, take selfies, and cheers, spinning around in circles on the shore, sure to get every angle possible. We got pictures with the ocean behind us, the shore, the cute little bungalow in the background, and even got one of all three of our toes in the sand.

Ana got a piece of seaweed stuck to her foot, and I literally thought I was going to pee myself running behind her as she panicked trying to get her foot free.

When I finally peel it off her skin, I run back to the ocean and dove underwater, only to come up with a different cluster of the green foliage stuck in my bottoms. Blake spits her drink out and screams.

Not quite the reaction I thought she'd have to my giant bush. It takes me a second to register, but when I do, I first notice the panic in her expression isn't aimed at me.

Time slows, flickering in fractured seconds as I catalogue everything around me, trying to place the source of her panic.

Blake's eyes are darting from one side to the other, her hand coming up and covering her mouth.

Ana drops her drink and takes off running.

"Luke," I scream. "Where the fuck is my brother?" As I pluck the remnants of my joke and throw the seaweed into the water, I turn around, surveying the situation. Counting heads.

Blake and Ana are on the shore with me.

Knox is jumping into the water.

Ty and Keith are both running across the deck of the boat.

Isa… I don't see Isa. Her head pops up from under her sun hat, and she, too, shrieks in panic.

"Where the fuck is my brother, Blake?"

"He's on the fucking boat, April. Will you please focus?"

Just then I see Luke dive into the water with a life preserver from the boat.

It all happened in a matter of seconds that feels like minutes until my gaze moves in the direction Luke and Knox are swimming and time slows even more.

Then it stops.

All of my senses heighten, and I can't breathe.

My hands go clammy.

I hear my heartbeat in my ears.

Heat radiates from my toes to my chest.

My vision blurs as tears cloud my line of sight.

I open my mouth to shout his name, but no sound comes out.

Cash.

Blake panicked and I assumed it was Luke. Cash didn't even cross my mind, not because I wasn't thinking of him but because I misread her reaction and my heart sank for my brother.

"Fuck the ocean!" Ana yells over her shoulder as her speed increases and without a second thought, I take off after her.

Before I can process what's happening, all three of us are sprinting down the shore toward Cash, who's drifting aimlessly on a boogie board straight toward a jagged cluster of rocks, where the waves are crashing violently.

"Cash!" I yell. "Holy fuck. He doesn't even realize he's in danger."

In a matter of seconds, one of the guides is on a jet ski moving in Cash's direction, slowing down just enough to grab the life preserver from Luke, while the other is urging the guys to come back to the boat and stay out of the way.

Cash turns just as the jet ski's roar swells behind him, and I stop cold, as if the world has yanked me out of my own body. I see it hit him, the realization. His eyes widen, not in fear, but in that awful, irreversible knowing. I scream his name, but the wind and waves steal it. The preserver hits the water near him and he grabs onto it just as the waves and rocks meet and the jet ski quickly roars as it changes direction.

He's gone, and with the waves crashing around him, I can't tell if he was able to grab on. My chest caves in. My legs won't move. The air feels thick, heavy, like I'm drowning without even touching the water.

All I can do is stand here as the horror of it swallows me whole.

Cash

April and Blake decided to head to the shore to hang out with Ana, so I used it as an excuse to take a break from snorkeling and cruise around on a boogie board.

I used to love riding tiny little waves on a boogie board when I was a kid. Surfing was never my thing, big waves scare the shit out of me, but the little butterflies that erupt in my stomach from being tossed around a bit in the water are a fond memory I have of days on the beach with my family.

I grew up in Vermont, but going on beach vacations was a yearly occurrence growing up.

Playing for the Sun Cats was a dream, because it meant I'd be close to the ocean. Little did I know having time to relax on the beach would not be in my schedule.

I can't do shit during the season, but it's mid January right now, and off season means my life is all mine.

"It's fucking beautiful out here," I whisper to myself.

I have literally never been anywhere this beautiful, not even the last time I came to Jamaica. This resort is next level. To be honest, one of the things that makes this place so serene and beautiful is the view I have of the sassy little blond who lives rent free in my head as I float around on this board.

I have been watching her bounce around the shore for the past 20 minutes, taking selfies with the girls and seeing her in her element is the only view I want to see. Her smile is bright enough to see from here, and her laughter carries in the sky, right along with Blake's scream.

Wait, why is Blake yelling?

I crane my neck to try to see April, but she's just standing there. Maybe there is a little sea creature crawling on the shore close to them.

I turn to look back out into the distance, loving how beautiful it is out here just to have my view obstructed by a jet ski. I try to move around him, but instead of a peaceful view, I'm met with the sight of an incoming jetty of rocks that was placed here to keep the waves from crashing onto the shore.

In a flash, I see a white life preserver coming at me from the jet ski and I grab it just as the engine whines and he takes off away from the rock structure.

The jolt of the jet ski pulls me under. Thank fuck for my baseball reflexes. I was able to catch it, otherwise my ass would be on the way to the hospital right now.

I would be on my way to the hospital, or worse.

This plays on repeat in my head as pain slices through my shoulder.

The pain is quick and intense. The moment the salt water kisses the open cut, it's like a blade of lightning carving through your skin, a sudden, electric flash of pain that sings like a scream underwater.

The more I focus on it, the sting blooms like fire in ice, sharp and merciless, as if the ocean itself has teeth and it's biting down, grinding salt into the wound with deliberate cruelty. It takes my breath away, and the sharp inhale from the pain allows water to invade my lungs.

Time slows. The world narrows until even the wind feels like it's made of knives as I come to the surface and gasp for air. But it's no use. As I strain for air, I'm sucked back into the water.

I could be on the way to the hospital, or worse. Maybe this is worse.

I repeat the words as I struggle to hold on to the life preserver. They are the only words that I think as flashes of her perfect face come one at a time in rapid fire through my mind.

Her perfect pink lips.

The honey blonde streaks in her hair.

Her perfectly tan skin, covered in freckles.

Eyes so blue they make the sky seem dull.

All I want is to see her face, and the pictures I've created of her in my mind keep the pain at bay as the water swirling around me turns red.

Will She Know

"Will she know how much I love her?"

- Garth Brooks

April

G YM SHORTS.

White t-shirt deliciously stretched out over his muscles. The brightest blue eyes in the entire world.

The image of Cash the very first time I saw him outside of Lit and Libations flashes in my mind so vividly I can see it as if he's standing in front of me. My heart pounds in response causing me to be stuck in a deep cleansing breath as if I'm trying to push the invasion of heartache away.

I close my eyes and take in another breath.

Perfect teeth.

Full lips.

Laugh lines around his eyes.

They are the first things I noticed when we were sitting across from one another at the bakery on our first fake date.

This memory sends the rest of them swirling like images on a carousel and I close my eyes to see them clearly, wanting to hold on to them like a warm hug.

Cash using the tip of his finger to take a drip of cheese off my lips and licking it clean.

Cash standing in front of me with a cart full of snacks just for me.

His eyes dancing wildly as he waits for me to type my response into his notes app.

Diner coffee. I smell it as if he's handing it to me right this second.

His eyes dilating and the bright blue seeming to shine a little brighter as he glances up at me from where he retreated between my thighs.

My breath hitches, and my throat constricts. It's all too much.

"Cash!" I yell, a screech of panic escaping my breath as my eyes fly open and I search for him.

"He's ok. He's ok." Ana reaches for my arm and pulls me in the direction of the rocks where Cash is now laying in the sand.

I take off running as fast as I can and crash into the sand next to him.

"Hey Tulip." He smiles, but the smile is strained, pain painting his features.

"You're hurt," I say, trying to push back a sob.

"I think one of the rocks caught my shoulder. I'll need some stitches, but other than that, I'm fine."

"You could have died, Cash. Died."

"But I didn't. This fucking guy right here, saved me," he says pointing towards Javon, one of our guides.

"Thank you," I say earnestly with a half smile to Javon.

"My lady, we have to take him to have this closed up. Will you be joining us?"

"No," Cash says with a stern tone. "She's squeamish."

How does he know that?

"Yes," I insist, ignoring his protest. "I need to make sure he's ok."

"We are just going to the medic over there." Javon points me in the direction of the little truck that just pulled up with the resort logo on the side.

Luke holds his shirt to Cash's wound, as he walks with us to the truck. He won't interject unless he needs to. It's not who he is. He would never tell someone how to do their job, but you can bet he'll be there to oversee everything they are doing to make sure it all checks out. If it doesn't he still won't say a word, he will just offer assistance.

I recall his humble demeanor as a doctor from a few years back when Mom got hit with a volleyball at one of those indoor volleyball courts when we visited Luke in Denver

He's so calm and stealthy in his approach, I didn't even notice him applying pressure and tending to Cash's wound on the beach.

I let the tension in my shoulders fall, knowing my big brother will make sure he's ok.

"No concussion, no broken bones, Ap. It's just a gnarly gash that needs to be cleaned really well and stitched." Luke smiles at me. "I checked him over myself."

He's ok. He's ok.

I take a long inhale.

He's ok.

Cash

"**Y**OU'RE A LUCKY MAN," Dr. Minto reassures me as he finishes placing the stitches on my shoulder. "The laceration is deep, but not as bad as I was expecting."

"I know, thank you."

Luke is sitting next. He's been right by my side since the jet ski pulled me away from the rocks. He was checking me over before the medic truck got to me. He has said very little, just observed every move meticulously.

I look over at him. "Thanks for coming, man."

"Don't sweat it. It's my job."

"It's not your job here, we're on vacation. For your wedding. You should be obsessing over your bride, not me." I offer him a coy smile. Grateful he tagged along. I was a little nervous about seeking medical attention at a resort in a foreign country.

"I'll go outside and update April, I know she's worried," he says as he walks out of the room.

I lay my head back on the exam table and take a deep breath.

"You should be good until you get home. The stitches inside will dissolve, but you will need to see your doctor in about 14 days to have the outer ones removed. They will look them over and decide if they need to stay in longer. No more pool or ocean." He smiles, adding, "But if you ignore my recommendation, here are some waterproof patches you can put over the wound to keep the water off it, you're lucky it's on your shoulder, just don't submerge it. Wash it twice a day, and right after being in the water. You have some bruising, so ice it and take it easy tonight. You will feel better tomorrow."

"Thanks again. I appreciate it." I grab the waterproof bandages and collect the rest of my belongings they brought in from the snorkel boat, and head out the door.

I know I was lucky, but close calls are not something new to me. I can't count the number of times I've almost taken a line drive to the head, tweaked my arm pitching, or slid and thought I took out my leg. Close calls are just that, close, but not final. I've learned not to focus on what could have been, and instead channel my energy into what is.

April, clearly doesn't share my view on this situation. She comes running the second I come into view.

"That bandage is huge. Are you ok? How big is the gash?" Her questions strike me with rapid fire and she's running out of breath.

"Take a breath." I kiss her on the forehead. "I'm ok. Luke said he was coming out here to tell you all was good."

"Yeah, well he sees some crazy ass shit, so I don't really trust his gauge of *fineness*."

"He's a doctor. I'm pretty sure he's used to not mincing his words. If it was bad, he'd tell you."

She rolls her eyes and starts taking things out of my hand.

"What do you think you're doing?" I ask with a laugh.

"You're hurt."

"You don't need to carry my stuff for me. I've had worse slide burn than this, babe. At least this got all stitched up." I offer her a smile and place my hand on the small of her back.

She looks up at me all doe-eyed and tries to force a smile.

Trying to comfort her, I place a kiss on her temple. "I'll make you a deal. You can tend to me all night." I wiggle my brow.

"Oh I will, just not the way you think." Her response is flat and void of emotion.

When the room to our door opens, she immediately starts the shower. "You get in and get all cleaned up, and then you can lay down and relax. I'll shower after you."

I want to protest. I want to invite her in with me, but I can tell she is rattled and all she needs is for me to be ok, so I do exactly as she asks.

The steam fills the bathroom, so I can't see the extent of my injury. But the warm water burns the few open scratches that surround the stitches. It feels just like slide burns I've had on my legs in the past.

I wasn't lying when I alluded to being happy it was bad enough for stitches. I've had burns so bad they sting for days. Plus, it's a bitch to take care of. You have to constantly clean and change out the dressing to avoid infection. Stitches are way less maintenance.

By the way the water burns as it slides down my right shoulder blade, I know shampoo will burn like a sonofabitch. I turn so I'm facing the water and slightly bend forward to rinse the shampoo from my hair.

When I turn back around, I get a glimpse of April through the large crack between the wall and the picture closing off the opening.

This time, my obstructed view of her is not nearly as entertaining. While I can't completely see her, I can tell she is hunched over with her face in her hands, and I recognize the slight wobble of her shoulders.

She is crying.

I hurry, slinging the towel around my waist and rush out of the bathroom. She is only a breath away, but the space between us feels vast, like a canyon carved by things unsaid.

I kneel down in front of her, placing my hand on her thigh, knowing full well my junk is inches from making an appearance.

"You are ghosting, Tulip," I say as I raise her chin so her eyes meet mine.

"I've been talking to you the entire time, how in the world am I ghosting you?"

"By not letting me in. You're here, but I feel like I'm with the ghost of you."

"I'm fine."

"You're not."

A sob escapes her, and I move next to her so I can pull her into my chest. It takes her a few minutes to start talking again, but when she does, she unloads all the fractured pieces floating around within her.

"Cash. You don't understand. I lost something before I even had the chance to fully want it, and then it almost happened again with you."

"What do you mean?" I am having a hard time following her.

"I can't have kids, Cash. Well, chances are so slim they'd call it a miracle. I went to the doctor after missing my period, and it spiraled into a series of appointments that resulted in me finding out I'm on the fast track to infertility. Premature Ovarian Failure. My body just quit. And nobody knows."

She pulls her knees to her chest and wraps her arms around them, protecting herself.

"I'm fine, until I'm not. Until someone starts talking about how *I'm next*. Someone at the wedding suggested that now that I have you, all we need next are kids, like it's some kind of invisible checkpoint."

"You've been walking around, carrying that alone? For how long, baby?" I am careful with my tone, I don't want her to retreat back into her shell.

"I don't want to be the sad story. The one who ruins someone else's future, but I'm letting myself do that with you. I'm letting my heart open, and then I almost lost you too. It's too much."

I breathe trying to break down all the shrapnel she just fired. Trying to untangle the web she's weaving between us.

"What scared you today?" It's a dumb question. I know the answer, but I think she needs to get it out.

"You were drifting into those rocks, and everyone was screaming, but I couldn't. I couldn't scream, I couldn't move. I couldn't even think. All I wanted to do was throw up." She wipes her nose with the back of her hand. "I didn't even get to decide I wanted you, before you were gone, pulled under the water, out of sight. Life keeps trying to make decisions for me without letting me be a part of it."

I look right at her, but she won't look back. "I'm right here."

"What if you fall for me? What if you want—" She cuts off her own words, her voice breaking.

"What I want is a chance with you. You get to decide what life you have. What your future holds. I don't hold that decision for you, Tulip. I just want a chance with you. Not a checklist, not a maybe someday. You. And if your heart is a little harder to reach because of all of this, I've got a long wing-span."

I lay us both down and settle her head on my chest. She clings to me, pulling me as close as she can. But when she buries her face in my chest and her tears soak my already damp skin, the feel of them burns me.

"You're allowed to break. You just don't have to do it alone anymore."

So Good, It Almost Hurts

"Tides are gonna turn with the pull of the moon, and I'm gonna love you"
-Cody Johnson, Carrie Underwood

April

HE CONSOLED ME UNTIL I felt steady, but I'm sure laying on his back was not comfortable. After the tears faded and I got my shit together, I grabbed him some ice, cleaned his stitches, and we watched *The Proposal* for the second time until he drifted off to sleep. I've been rubbing his head for the past hour while the movie finished, afraid if I stop he'll stir.

I decided today, even though we have not explicitly said what we are doing here, I want to give it a try. I'm tired of losing before I start.

The room is quiet, except for the sound of the waves crashing on the beach outside our open sliding door. The breeze feels good. This is the perfect time to read. I turn the movie off and grab my Kindle.

My therapist suggested that I immerse myself in books and movies that are centered around pregnancy as well as unconventional family structures. She insists that becoming comfortable with someone having a baby in a fictional setting where I can work though my feelings in a low stakes situation will make real life situations more bearable. I had a really hard time being around Ana both times she was pregnant.

When my cousin had a baby last year, it almost broke me. That's when I decided I needed to work through my shit.

I know it's just a matter of time before Luke and Blake start trying for a baby. The thought brings mixed emotions. I get excited by the idea of seeing my brother as a father, my best friend caring for a baby, my parents becoming grandparents. Then the guilt sets in, I might not ever get to offer them that same gift.

However, the salt stings just as hard when the wound is fictional. I get to the part of the book where the main character is holding her baby, skin to skin after birth and the reality that I may never get that experience makes my heart sink. I know there are many ways to become a mother, but feeling my baby grow inside me is a fleeting dream. Each time my period fails to come, it's a sharp reminder that my window is closing.

I click my Kindle off and lay in the silence, Cash's arm draped across me listening to the waves outside. I think back to the day, three years ago that I found out.

You have a condition called Premature Ovarian Failure.

That sentence replays over and over in my head. Every. Single. Day.

I have never told a soul, not even my mother. My body literally is losing the ability to do what it was designed to do. I already live in this constant state of racing the clock, and my family wants me to find love so badly, I can't bring myself to give them one more reason to wait for me to find love.

It makes this entire fake relationship with Cash seem so much easier than facing the truth. I push men away.

Shit.

How in the world are Cash and I supposed to be a real couple trying to be a fake couple playing a real couple?

My thoughts remind me of the episode from Friends, *"They don't know that we know that they know that we know?"*

I break out in hysterical laughter, another realization hitting me just as Cash wakes.

"What's so funny, Tulip?"

"Sorry, I didn't mean to wake you." I jump at his words.

"Don't be. I love the sound of your laughter. It's so much better than your tears. Hit me, I'd love to know what makes you laugh in the middle of the night."

I replay my entire thought process for him and he chuckles. "I'm glad you're finding humor in the small things, babe. Can I hold you?"

"Sure, but can we lose the comforter? I get really hot."

Without hesitation he pushes it to the foot of the bed and pulls me in tight.

"Are you sure this doesn't hurt you?" I ask.

"Not even a little. It makes it feel so much better."

Just like that, we're an actual couple. It wasn't this big to-do, just unfolded naturally. Nothing like the movies at all.

"Cash," I say, wanting to make sure we are on the same page.

"Yeah?"

"We're getting really good at this relationship thing. I wish it was real."

"It is real, Tulip. You just needed a little time to catch up."

Cash

WE BOTH CRASHED PRETTY quickly and cuddled all night with my arm draped over her, pulling her in tight as I lay behind her. We stayed like this all night. Neither one of us moved.

Thankfully, we were positioned so my right shoulder covered in stitches was not on the mattress.

I've been awake for a few minutes when she stirs to life.

"Morning," I say in her ear.

"You held me all night?"

"There was not a chance in hell I was letting you go." I pull her even closer than she already is. "Listen," I say as I inhale the faint smell of brown sugar. "You said you wished this was real. You meant that right?"

She turns so she is facing me, laying flat on her back, "I did."

"Good," I say, running my fingers slowly up and down the flat of her stomach. My fingers glide gently over her soft skin, and with each swipe of my touch I glide them farther and farther north.

"Hhhh." Her breath hitches as I graze the underside of her beast.

I slowly move my fingers so they dance back around her belly button, as I lay long slow kisses over her shoulder that's peeking out of the collar of her sleep shirt.

She moves her hand so it lays over mine and gently guides it back up her skin.

My kiss traces the curve of her shoulder, as I trace her pulse, working my way up her jawline.

She brings her hand up to my chin, pulling me towards her and as my lips close in on hers, the pads on my fingers hover in a featherlike touch over her nipple.

"Fuck," I take in a deep breath before crashing my lips to hers.

Our kiss is deep and warm.

Slow.

Nothing about this is hurried.

Not wanting to break our kiss, now that I have it I can't stop it, I reposition myself so I am hovering above her. My rock hard cock pushes into the warm space between her legs.

"Mmmm," she moans, causing my featherlike dance over her breast to turn hard and needy. I kneed her tit in my hand and then pinch and pull her nipple as I devour her mouth.

She shimmies so her hand can wiggle between our bodies, and when her delicate hand falls around my cock, it jumps in response. She just holds it for a second as if she's studying the size before she starts to gently pump her hand up and down the length.

"Cash." She pulls her lips away from mine just enough to speak.

"Hmmm."

"My hand is dry."

"Ok." Our lips barely part.

"I need to wet it, or it won't feel good."

"How do you want to do that, Tulip?"

She ignores my question and pushes me onto my back. Without hesitation she slides me into her mouth and my hips rock into her as I feel the head of my dick tickle the back of her throat. She didn't waste any fucking time.

"Ap… April." I breathe, "You don't hav—"

She pulls back and looks me straight in the eyes.

"Cash, I don't do anything I don't want to, especially in bed. I have wanted your cock in my mouth for too long."

She returns her mouth and licks a long slow path from the base of my balls to the head of my dick just before she slides me back inside.

She pumps me in and out of her perfect fucking mouth a few times before she pulls away and spits on the tip just before sliding it back in.

"Fuck, babe," I draw out my words over a strained moan. "You are really good at this."

She smiles at me, and I'm a goner.

I sit up and pull her onto me so I can hook my fingers into the waistband of her panties as I place kisses over her collarbone.

I slide them down and she readjusts so I can get them off.

"Cash," she whispers, but it's not a seductive whisper. There is pain behind it.

"What's wrong?" I stop everything and pull my hands away from her skin.

"No," she says, placing my hands back on her. "You need to know that my condition makes this a little tricky." She winces.

"Ok." My words are soft and slow. "Are you ok?"

"My body is on fire, and I am so turned on, but I'm not ready."

"Ok. We stop," I say.

"What? No. That's not what I mean. I have a really hard time getting *wet*." The last word tapers off her tongue like it pains her.

"Oh, baby that is the best news." I roll her onto her back and hover over her. "That just means you need me to devour you. Worship you. Explore every inch of that perfect pussy until you are dripping."

"You don't mind?"

"Fuck no, I have never wanted anything more."

I move my way down her body until my lips are a whisper above her pussy. "I don't want to fuck this up, baby."

I open my mouth and lay my tongue flat over her clit, licking it like my favorite ice cream cone, in repetitive strokes as I slowly insert two fingers inside her.

At first she is a little dry, so I take my fingers and slowly raise them to her lips for a little lubrication.

She takes my fingers into her mouth without question, rolling her tongue around them in slow circles.

"Shit," I moan.

I pull my fingers out of her mouth and she releases them with a little pop.

This time my fingers slide into her with ease, and I fall into a perfect rhythm of licking her clit and curling my fingers in just the right spot.

It causes her walls to contract slightly, pulling away from me, and then… there it is. She's dripping for me.

"Ca-Cash. Oh shit!" she screams.

"Don't come yet, Tulip. You are going to soak my dick."

Knowing we are on borrowed time, I hurry off of her to grab a condom.

"No," she says in a heavy pant. "I—" Her eyes lower. "We don't need that, unless it makes you more comfortable."

"Are you sure?" I ask.

"It's a little scary, but I want you to have me, all of me." She's trembling, but it's not out of fear. It's anticipation.

She looks away when she says it, and I see it in her eyes. The way grief and hope sit side by side. She's not saying no to protection. She's saying yes to something bigger.

I stop moving and lower myself on top of her looking her in the eyes as I slowly slide inside her.

I kiss her neck and can feel her pulse against my lips. She moves to make room for me and I feel my balls tighten.

"Tulip. Don't move," I say.

"What?"

"I've. I've never been bare before. This feels so—" I pull out just a little, "This feels so fucking good, I'm about to come."

"Cash, if we don't move I'm going to dry out, and this will be over before we even start."

"I just need a second, baby. If you do, that's what my mouth is for."

Without moving my hips, I slowly roll my fingers over her clit, rolling the evidence of her arousal over it, proving to her that she's ok.

I roll my fingers at a steady pace until her hips start to rock, and her walls begin to tighten. That's when I move.

In and out in long slow strokes, biting the inside of my lip until my taste buds find the faintest metallic flavor of blood dancing across them.

She stills slightly and her breath quickens as her walls close in around me and I feel her dripping around my balls. Then I lose it, spilling inside her.

"Mmmm." Her moans are low and strained.

"You are perfect, Tulip."

Love Out Loud

April

I'VE NEVER DARED TO allow myself the simple pleasure of love. I know to most it doesn't seem simple, but right now, with Cash, it feels like it could be. Being with him feels simple.

"You have a condition called Premature Ovarian Failure."

Those words branded my heart. Scared it. It sent me down a slip and slide of emotion I didn't want to burden anyone with, not even my parents. I have been carrying this secret for years, avoiding love, avoiding sex via blowjobs, not wanting to let anyone near my heart in fear they would want kids one day. Also, the veil of fear that my body would not cooperate and my secret would be out. Life already made the decision for me, but it seems cruel to make that choice for someone else.

I will have a family one day when I'm ready, but it will not be one born out of the traditional sense. It may not include babies that share my DNA, or a partner to raise them with, but they will hold my entire heart.

"What's swirling around in that pretty little head of yours, Tulip?" Cash surprises me, walking up behind me in the shallow water as I float on a donut in the pool.

"Honestly?" I ask.

"Always." Cash smiles at me, and his eyes shine so bright.

"I was thinking how simple being with you is. It's effortless, even when everything else seems less simple," I say, standing now in the middle of the tube.

He bends his knees so he is shoulder deep, careful to keep his bandage above water, and reaches beneath the tube and slides his hands up my waist and plays with the waistband on my swim bottoms, rolling his thumb over my skin over and over. I press myself into his touch, leaning back on the donut between us.

"Your skin is so soft." He smiles into the crook of my neck, running slow kisses up and down my neck as we float in the pool. "I love the feel of your skin on mine."

"Cash, we are in the pool, and my family is somewhere around here." I laugh.

"I'll behave. I just can't keep my hands off you, baby." His words hit my ear in a whisper as he lays one palm flat over my stomach and trails it along my skin, until the tip of his thumb dances below my top and grazes the underside of my breast. The touch sends a shiver down my spine.

"You are so fucking responsive to my touch," he groans in my ear.

"Hey guys," Blake says louder than necessary as Ana, Knox, and Luke approach.

She gives me a sideways smile and plops into a tube next to me.

"Have you been here long?" Luke asks and I see his eyes flash to Cash's hand splayed across my stomach. To say my brother is protective is an understatement.

"Not too long." I smile.

Instead of sliding away from Cash's touch, I sink into it, placing my hand over his and lacing our fingers together.

"Do you want a drink?" Cash asks.

"A dirty banana sounds amazing right now." I smile.

"Oh, that sounds great! Get three, please," Ana calls over to Cash as he starts to head towards the bar.

"How does it feel to be a Jennings?" I ask Blake with a smile.

"I feel like I've kind of always been a Jennings, but being Luke's wife is amazing." Her smile is so bright, I can't help but smile back.

I've always wanted a sister, and couldn't think of a better one than Blake.

"So," she continues, "I want you two to be the first to know." Her smile grows. Her eyes dance like she's keeping a secret the stars would envy. "We decided last week that once we get back home, we are going to start trying for a baby."

Ana screams in excitement, and the two of them start jumping up and down.

For a moment, I let myself believe that I'll get to hold a baby someday. Then I feel the familiar ache bloom. The one that reminds me about the body I live in.

I close my eyes and swallow the thought, deciding to live in *this* moment. I get to be an aunt. Something else I have always wanted.

Butterflies erupt in my stomach and my heart starts beating out of my chest. My entire body gets warm and I realize as I erupt in excitement that I'm not sure there will be anything more exciting than being an aunt.

"Oh my god! You are going to have the cutest babies. Can you imagine your freckles and full lips on a baby with Luke's dark coloring? Or Luke's honey colored eyes with your red hair. Oh, or maybe the baby will take after their auntie with blond locks," I say with a smile.

"Luke has been so excited that he has already started looking into the hospital daycare. He said he's been visiting it at random times to see what they do at different times of the day."

"Do you think he's going to go as feral over you as Knox does when I'm pregnant?" Ana asks and the question is not one I want the answer to.

"You know what, that sounds like a great conversation for the two of you to have while I go see if the guys need help carrying the drinks."

After about 2 hours in the pool, and too many cocktails, I decided to retreat to the shade for a little break and a poolside nap.

Only problem, I am not getting a restful nap with this digital Cash Easton rabbit hole I've found myself falling down. Heart first, spinning with heart pumping images of the man keeping me company every night. My heart races. It feels like the blood is rushing out of my veins, pooling between my legs with every scroll.

There was a video of him at the plate, waiting for the pitch. His jaw ticked as the ball flew a little close to his elbow and he had to take a little jump back to get out of the path of the ball. That small motion was all it took to get me worked into a frenzy.

But I didn't stop there, I watched video after video of him making small motions, gestures that sent me reeling. He was in an interview and an older lady yelled his name from the stands behind him, and the small wink and smile he gave her melted me.

It gets me thinking, he's not just any baseball player, he is the star of the Sun Cats, across the country. How in the hell are we supposed to make this work? I mean, I don't even know anything about baseball, let alone their training schedule.

I make a mental note to get all the details I need from Knox in a nonchalant way.

But my thoughts are interrupted when Cash lays down next to me on the small lounger.

"Damn, you're just over here checking out fine ass men while I'm eyeing you from the pool. Rude." He laughs.

"I'm trying to learn more about what you do," I explain, honestly.

"I play baseball, babe. It's not really rocket science."

"Cash, I don't know anything about baseball. I've literally never been to a game."

He sits up and his motion is so fast, I almost fall off the chair.

"What?" He laughs, "Oh man. You have to come to opening day. It's the best day there is! You can sit with my parents in the suite. You'll love it!"

"Do I at least get to meet you parents before then?" I chuckle. "I would really like you to be there when I meet them, not down on the field, making me drool."

He smiles, and again I am taken aback by how effortless and natural this all is. "They actually don't live far, only about 40 minutes from the hospital. You can meet them whenever you want, Tulip."

"So, we're really doing this?" I ask.

"Yes." He places a kiss on my forehead and lays back down with me on the lounger, and seconds later, we both fall asleep.

Cash

"WHAT ARE YOU GOING to order?" I ask April as she scans over the menu for the third time.

"I don't know, it all looks so good." She bites her bottom lip and I reach across the table and run my thumb across her chin.

"Don't do that, Tulip."

"Sorry. It's how I think."

"Noted. Only give you complex decisions when I can be buried deep inside you," I tease. "You know, this is all inclusive, you can ask them to bring you samples of all the things you think look good, and make your own little buffet style plate," I tell her as I look over the menu one more time.

"They'll do that?" Her eyes grow wide.

"You just have to request it."

That's exactly what we do. I wanted to do something special for April, something for just the two of us, a real first date. What better way to spend our first official date than a private dinner for two under the stars.

April is sitting across from me taking small bites of each item on the many plates of food that were brought to our table. Her hair is slicked back into a tight bun so I have a perfect view of her pink lips.

I settle into my chair, feeling the ocean breeze on my skin. As darkness unfolds, the first stars emerge overhead like delicate pinpricks of light reflecting across the water's surface.

The aroma of the sea mingles with the scents of lemon-dressed salad, grilled seafood, and fresh herbs. As I sip wine, a contented warmth blooms inside me. This is what I've been waiting for.

"What's your favorite?" she asks, pulling me out of my daze.

"The lobster is amazing. What about you?"

"Coco bread. I need to learn how to make it when I get home. I've never had it, but I think I could make it."

"It would be the perfect crowd craving," I finish her thought without even realizing it. She smiles at me, and we finish our meal in the most comfortable silence I have ever experienced.

A gentleman comes over and carves two giraffes out of a small piece of drift-wood with a heart in the middle that he paints red.

"A gift, my lady," he says as he hands April the carving.

Staring across the table from my girl, the only sounds that can be heard are the waves crashing in the distance, and in this moment, I feel like this is what love must feel like.

"Cash," she says, breaking the silence as we make our way back to the room.

"Yeah, baby."

"I don't even know what your schedule is like. How do other players make long distance work?"

"Every relationship is a little different, but there are a lot of players that live in different cities than they play for. Our season is long, March to October, sometimes November. But, we have breaks and long weekends, and they travel home. Sometimes their families travel to games. You'd be surprised how well it works."

"You seem so sure." She smiles, but I can tell the idea is weighing on her.

"I'm sure I want to keep seeing you." I kiss her hand. "Let's take it one day at a time, and worry about things as they arise. I don't want us to spend all of our time together worried about what happens when we are apart."

"I'll try," she assures me, and I believe her.

I take her hand and bring it to my lips, placing small delicate kisses over the top of her hand, her wrist, inhaling my way up her arm until I reach her neck.

We are on a secluded path that leads to our room. It's late, and there are a few trees in the corner of the path, just out of reach of the lights.

I gently guide her into the shadows and turn her so her back is against me.

"What are we doing in the dark, Cash," she asks, curiosity lacing her voice.

I tilt her chin up to the sky, "Watching the stars."

They are bright, like a canvas of dust floating overhead.

"You see all those stars twinkling?"

"Yes."

"They're thousands of miles away, but when you look at them they feel like they're right here, we're so attached to them, we don't even think about how far they are."

I continue placing little kisses along her neck, slowly moving across her jawline. I kiss the space just behind her ear as the tips of my fingers dance across her stomach.

Slowly tracing circles on her skin, I continue, "You and me, Tulip, we will be the same."

"Mmm." She nods her head in response, but no words come out, just a tiny little hum as my fingers move dangerously close to the hem of her palazzo pants. I gently tug the string, tied at her waist.

"I bet, if you looked up, the stars look just the same back in Vermont as they do here." I slowly move my hand beneath her waistband and still.

"You don't have panties," I groan in her ear.

"You could see the outline through the fabric," she teases.

"Fuck me," I moan as I slide my hand farther down until I am met with the slickness between her legs.

My fingers run over her clit with a featherlike touch, and she moans. I quickly take my other hand and place it over her mouth to silence her.

"Baby, you have to keep quiet, or someone will hear us, and we will have to stop."

"Don't stop," she pants against my palm.

I take that as a directive, and slide my fingers inside her hot wet cunt.

With one hand I pull my shirt off, wanting to feel any tiny bits of her skin on mine. After sitting on the small wall, I pull her down on my lap. I take a moment to take in the smell of sugar, sand, and sunscreen as I gently pull her tank top up, freeing her nipple. I roll it between my fingers until it is firm beneath my touch.

"Look at the stars, baby. Memorize them while my fingers fuck this beautiful pussy. Come all over my hand."

"Mmmm," she moans louder, but it comes out muffled, as she squeezes her lips together.

"They don't seem that far do they, baby?"

"No," her voice is ragged and soft, soft enough that I loosen my grip just a touch. I curl my fingers and rub the palm of my hand over her clit as I pump them in and out of her. A light sheen of sweat covers her forehead as I place a kiss there. Her body tightens, and her breaths become shallow.

"Come on my hand, baby."

I lightly bite her earlobe, and the slight mix of pleasure and pain sends her over the edge. Her body quakes, and I have to move my hand from her mouth and wrap it around her body, pulling her close to me as she goes slack.

"Distance means nothing baby when the same stars shine on us both."

The Sting

"The look in your eyes like a window, the taste of your kiss soaked in wine"

-Carly Pearce

April

"I'm going to go have coffee with the girls before we leave for the airport." Cash is still in bed, half asleep as I place a kiss on his lips.

"Don't be too long, I might miss you." He smiles. He has one of those smiles, a little crooked, so imperfect, it's perfect.

"Go back to sleep, and it will feel like I was only gone for a second."

When I get outside, the air is damp and thick, and feels warmer than it has the entire trip, almost uncomfortable.

Blake and Ana are in the same area, so it's no surprise that we all meet up on the path leading to the restaurant.

"You look well rested," Ana jokes as I approach.

"Yeah, well sharing a bed with someone does that to me I guess. I don't know what I'm going to do when Cash goes back to Cali."

"He's gone back a few times since you started dating, right?" Blake asks.

Shit. That's right.

This is silly.

"Actually," I start, thinking back to the day this all started.

I remember standing outside his Airbnb, heart in my throat, asking him to come with me. He barely hesitated, and I should have known that all my preconceived notions about him were wrong.

"About that." All of a sudden my palms are sweaty, and my heart is racing. "Cash and I were not dating."

Both Ana and Blake stop and simultaneously turn to face me. Neither one of them says a word, but their faces morph into something between confusion and disbelief.

I take their silence as an opportunity to continue.

"It was complete chance that we walked into L&L together, we most certainly weren't dating regardless of what Luke assumed. After that night, I never really thought about him again, until we went to dinner at my parent's and mom brought it up. You were all so sure we were dating, no one really let me say a thing, and I got so frustrated I just went with it. I showed up at Cash's apartment and begged him to come here as my date."

They both just stare at me, I have no idea what to say, or how to proceed.

After a few seconds Ana interjects, "You look so *happy*, like, hold on… he looks at you like you hung the fucking moon, April. Are you sure he doesn't have feelings for you?"

"He does. I do. We—" I start fumbling my words. "Something happened here, we accidentally had sex one night, and it changed everything."

Blake bursts out laughing, breaking the blank stare passing between us, "How the fuck do you accidentally have sex? We can come back to everything else you just unloaded in a second, I have to hear this."

I cringe, not believing I am divulging this. "I had a dream that we were having sex, and I woke up to him inside me. Then I panicked because I was pretty sure I had an 'O' and was in a sleep haze and missed it. Long story short, he was not having it, and made sure I got off again and remembered it."

"That is so fucking hot," Ana says, fanning herself.

I turn to look at Blake, "I'm really sorry I lied. I'll tell Luke later."

Blake's face falls flat, and I can tell she's contemplating how Luke will react.

"Ap, I'm sorry I didn't listen to you and you felt like you had to make up this lie, but please, don't tell Luke. He's just getting to the point where he is seeing all Cash has to offer, and if he thinks for one second he's taking advantage of you or anything like that he will lose his shit. I'll clue him in when we get home, after you two have been dating a while."

"Yeah, that's probably a better plan," I sigh in relief.

"Ok, what in the hell were you going to do if you didn't start dating?" Ana laughs.

"We were going to somehow stage a break up at the airport on the way home." I shrug, realizing now how insanely ridiculous it all sounds.

I put my hands over my face and take a deep breath, "Ok, let's go get coffee! I need a lot of caffeine to endure the interrogation that's about to ensue."

Cash

"IT'S A LITTLE SCRATCH. Barely even a cut," I try to explain to Coach on the phone. I had to report the injury, even though it was minor, it's in my contract. The Sun Cats own my body, it's just the way it is, and the scar would be something the team doctor would notice in my pre-season check up, and I could lose my contract if I didn't report it. I filled out the form this morning, and sure as shit, Coach was on the phone with me less than five minutes later.

"I don't give a shit how insignificant you think it is, you are in another country. What if it's infected from all the pool water and shit. Watch later today Cash, even though it's all adults at that resort, bet not one of those motherfuckers leaves the pool to piss." I cringe at his accurate assessment. "I'll have Natalie call the airline and change your flight. The team doctor will see you after you land *here* in San Diego."

"I have so much work coming up with the foundation. Can't I just get cleared from a doctor in Vermont? I'm volunteering at a hospital. There are plenty of amazing doctors who can clear me."

"You don't have a lot to do there any more. I already have Natalie on the phone with the foundation telling them you won't be back. Baseball comes first, Cash. You signed a contract. This is not something I should have to explain to you." He doesn't even wait for my response, he hangs up.

"Fuck!" I yell and throw my phone onto the bed, just in time for it to ping. A notification from the airline lights up my screen.

I pace the room before slamming my suitcase on the bed. I need to pack up all of this shit to prepare for what I can only assume will be the first flight out of here tomorrow morning.

I walk into the bathroom to grab my swimsuit I left drying on the line in the shower and when I open I pause and inhale the faint smell of brown sugar. Her scent clings to the air, soft and familiar.

San Diego. I have to go back to San Diego. She has a business, a life in Vermont, and I have to go back to San Diego. The name of a place I love burns my tongue as I silently mouth the words, trying to decide what this really means to us, how this actually does work. I tried to convince her it would be ok when she asked. I tried to reassure her that this is common, and it is, but I've never paid attention to *how* my teammates make it all work. I've never had a reason to.

I can't sit here and live in the constant state of what ifs. It will make me fucking crazy. I grab my suit off the line and walk back out into the room. I pick up all of my clothes that have been discarded around the room in heated undressing and place them into a hamper bag I always carry in my suitcase.

I refold all of the clothes I bought that I never wore, and neatly stack my toiletries on the counter so I can easily pack them in the morning.

Ding.

An email flashes on my screen from the airline just as another email pops up from Natalie. I see the entire brief message on my screen, so there is no need to open the actual email.

> Flight is rebooked. You should get an email with your reservation. Your connection in Dallas has a brief layover, enough time for food.
> Natalie

Natalie never has been one to mince words, straightforward and to the point. Even personal interactions with her are cold and brief. You'd never guess she was thirty-something surrounded by professional athletes.

I open the email from the airline and am pleasantly surprised that my flight leaves an hour after the one April will be on, and is in the same terminal. At least I can see her off.

"What are you doing?" April says with wide eyes as she opens the door. I can see the worry in her expression as she surveys the room, talking in my neatly packed suitcase open on the bed.

"Coach just called. They're sending me back to San Diego from here to get cleared. I was packing just in case I had an early flight in the morning."

"Ok," she says with a soft smile. "That makes sense. They want to make sure you will be ready to play in a few weeks. Damn. I just thought we'd get a little more time."

"He cancelled my contract with the foundation," I blurt the words out, not wanting to hide it from her for even a second.

Her smile falls. "What does that mean?"

"Means that as far as the Sun Cats are concerned, I'll have no reason to go back to Vermont."

Too Good To Be True

"That lonesome feeling comes to my door, and the whole world turns blue…"
–Brooks and Dunn, Kacey Musgraves

April

"HERE IS A COFFEE and a croissant for the ride. I also have a small grocery order with a few essentials being delivered. It should be there shortly after you get home." He kisses me, and the weight of the impending distance between us is debilitating.

"Cash, you di—" He puts his lips on mine again to silence me.

"I want to. It's going to be late. I will FaceTime you as soon as I get home after my appointment."

"Ok." My voice is weak and strangled.

"I also had Natalie call and move your seat so you can visit with your mom on the way home.

He is the kindest man I have ever been with. I offer him a soft smile with a thank you, I wish there could be a promise of things to come. Cash and I had enough sex last night to hold most people over for months, but he is my newest addiction, and I'm not sure I'll make it this undetermined amount of time.

"I'll talk to you soon, Tulip."

"Ok." I have a million feelings brewing inside me, but this is the only word I can manage to let escape without tears.

"It's going to be ok, baby. He will get checked out by the team doctor, and I'm sure after some time passes, he will be able to convince them to let him come check in on the foundation. Your brother said they didn't pull the partnership, just Cash," my mom tries to reassure me, but Cash seemed pretty confident that this was a final decision. The MLB doesn't take situations like this lightly.

We are about an hour into the flight, and I feel like right now, while probably not the best, is a good enough time for me to clear the air with my parents and let them know what has been going on. Only, I look over and my dad is snoring with his headphones in. Guess I can talk to him later.

"Mom."

"Yeah?" her voice is always so cheery.

"I have to tell you something, and I really need you to let me finish before you say anything."

"Is everything ok?"

"I think so." I take a deep breath trying to find the words that often escape me. I'm so nervous, I'm sure the entire plane can hear my heartbeat pounding against my chest. My hands are slick with sweat, my throat is dry, and every little sound in the quiet plane feels like it is echoing off my bones. "Mom, Cash and I are in such a great place, we are falling fast for each other, but, mom, when we came here we were not actually together. I tried to tell you, but you were so insistent that Blake and Luke needed to give us a shot, and seemed so happy that I had someone, I didn't know how to tell you. I asked him to join me as my fake boyfriend, but the more we got to know each other, real feelings started to develop.

"I'm glad you are happy." She smiles, and then sits back in her chair and takes a sip of her Diet Coke.

"Mom!" I exclaim, frustrated that she didn't seem to hear me, again.

"April, we are on a plane, and people are sleeping. I am not stupid honey. I know there have been many times over the years you and your brother think we are, but I promise you. While I might be a lot of things, stupid is not one. I know you were not together, but Luke told me how he talked about you at the hospital, and the look in his eyes. I saw his eyes on you at the grand opening. There was a little spark, so I played into it, hoping you would bring him to dinner at our house to appease me. I didn't quite think you would go to this length to avoid a hard conversation and bring him to another country, but it worked out. He adores you, sweetie."

"Mom! That is terrible," I scold her in a hushed whisper.

"No, it's meddling. Sometimes a mom has to meddle. In this case it worked out. Now tell me the other thing you have been hiding."

I look at her confused, wondering how in the hell she knows I have been hiding something else.

"I was diagnosed with a condition that has caused my ovaries to prematurely stop producing hormones," I blurt it out, because I know if I think about it for even a second, I'll avoid the conversation completely.

Her voice is calm and soothing as she speaks, "What do you know about it?"

She always asks the right question to get me talking. "It could decrease my life expectancy by two years at most, there is a very small chance I could still have babies, but at this point it would be considered a medical miracle and eventually no longer be a possibility at all. In the last 9 months or so, my hormones have depleted so much, I take hormone replacements. They are starting to help, and the doctor said at my age, they will eventually make the symptoms almost undetectable. That's about all there is to know."

She closes her eyes for a second and I can see the silent wince in her expression. "How long have you known?"

I know this is hurting her. And I am about to hurt her even more. We're way too close for me to have hid this from her for so long. This is not the relationship we have, but facing things head on has never been a strength of mine. I need to do better, so I'm starting today.

"About 4 years ago. My periods started getting sporadic, I thought it was my birth control. Turns out the hormones in my birth control were making it worse, so I stopped taking it. It took a few months to diagnose, but I really struggled with the finality of it, and I didn't know how to say the words out loud. No one knows. Well, Cash knows. But other than him, I've never spoken a word about it. Every time I tried the words never came, only emotion."

She looks at me with tears in her eyes and pulls me into a side hug, running her fingers through my hair as my head rests in the crook of her shoulder. "I hate that you carried that alone."

"I'm sorry," I say.

"Don't be. This is your news to share when you are ready. There are no expectations from us." She takes a moment before she continues, and when she does I can hear the smile in her voice, "You love him."

"Mom, we have literally been together, days. Days. Not months, days."

"Again, there are no expectations, no guidelines, April. You have a secret that you didn't tell a soul, not me, dad, Luke, or Blake. But you told him." She smiles, "You needed him to know. You wanted him to know."

"My body made a decision for me, I can't make that for him."

"Exactly." She smiles again. Why does she keep smiling? "You see a future with him, and want him in on the secret."

I think about her assessment, and can't find an argument.

"April, you love him."

<h1 style="text-align:center;">Cash</h1>

"**W**HAT WERE YOU THINKING?" Coach scolds from across his desk.

The doctor cleared me, the stitches will come out in 12 days, and there is no sign of infection.

"I was thinking floating on a boogie board was safer than riding a water bike or surfing." Now is not the time to be a smart ass, but I can't help it. It's how I cope with any type of emotion, and right now I have a lot of them.

"You could have lost your contract, just to shmooze the doctor supervising you."

"You know how important this foundation work is to me. You know how much I want to see this take off, how much I wish there was a place like this for Knox," I yell, now unable to contain my emotions.

"It's not your job, Cash, this is. This is your fucking job, and you get paid the big bucks to be healthy and play baseball."

"It's a cut. I could cut myself with a kitchen knife cooking dinner." My tone is far more disrespectful than it should be, "I'm sorry. I just… I wanted to see it take off. It needs the backing from the MLB."

"It has it, Cash, just not from you." He stands and opens the door signaling our conversation is over.

As promised, I pick up my phone to FaceTime April.

It only takes one ring for her face to fill the screen, and all of the tension in my muscles melt away.

"How did it go?" she asks. The room is dark, so I know she's already in bed and the thought kills me. I should be there.

"No infection. Stitches will come out in 12 days, just like Luke said." I smile, but it doesn't reach my eyes.

"What's wrong?" Her voice is sleepy.

"Nothing, Coach is just concerned. How was your flight?"

"I told my mom about us, about my condition."

I'd decided to lay down in my bed before I called her, but this caused me to sit up, wanting a better look at her face.

"How did that go?"

"Really good. I should have told her from the start."

"There is no standard way to handle stressful situations, Tulip. Anyone who holds expectations of you, is not in your corner."

She smiles, "That's what my mom said."

"She's a smart lady." I take a breath, "I already miss you."

"Same."

"Hey, did you get a package today?" I ask, knowing it was delivered about ten minutes ago, but not wanting to be too obvious in changing the subject.

"No?" she says skeptically.

"Yes you did. Go check outside your door. I left delivery instructions to leave it there, and not in the mailbox." I smile at her, waiting for her to move.

She slowly gets out of bed and I see her shimmying as she slides a hoodie over her body and moves towards her door, sets the phone down, so I can't really see her anymore.

"You get it, Tulip?"

"Yes, just getting ready to open it."

"Can you prop me up so I can see?" I laugh.

"Shit, sorry! I'm nervous," she says walking back into her dark room, but my attention is stolen by the hoodie she pulls back off as she sits back down in her bed.

"Why are you nervous? It's from me. I promise you will like it." I smile again trying to convince her she should be anything but nervous.

"I've never gotten a mystery package delivered before. Everything that comes here is ordered by me." She smiles now, and while skeptical, I can see the excitement.

"Hhhh!" a sharp gasp escapes her lips as she lifts the dildo from the box. "One, this is huge. Two, why does it have horns?"

I bark a laugh, caught off guard by her description. "Tulip, that is the exact same size as my dick, I double checked. And the *horns,* as you call them, are massagers that stimulate the lower part of your clit that extends just inside."

She looks confused.

"Baby, your clit extends into the vaginal canal, and when it's massaged, it feels amazing." I look her in the eye through the phone so she knows I'm not fucking with her.

"How do you know this shit?" she jokes.

"Pussy is one thing I have dedicated my life to becoming an expert of."

"So cocky," she teases. "Prove it."

She pulls the hoodie off and the blankets up.

"What are you doing?" I ask, wishing I could be there to see her in person.

"You know I sleep naked at home. I told you that," she laughs.

"Show me." My words are short and demanding.

I half expected her to protest, but she doesn't, she props the phone up on what I assume is her nightstand and kneels on the bed in front of the camera, giving me the perfect view of her body.

"Shit," I groan, adjusting my pillows behind me so I can have a comfortable view. "Touch yourself, baby."

She looks at me with a raised brow, but slowly slides her fingers over her nipples, making them harden with contact.

"Lower," I demand.

She does as I ask, lowering her hand until it hovers just over her clit. Her breath stutters and it only makes me wish I was there with her, and it was me touching her instead of her touching herself. The sight though, is perfection. I am definitely going to have to ask her to do this again when I'm with her.

"Cash," she moans my name and it breaks my thoughts of what's to come. I miss her. This isn't enough. I need her heartbeat against mine. "I— I can't ever do this on my own. Tell me what to do."

"Fuck, Baby. You are going to make me come if you keep talking like that." I spit in my hand and rub it up and down the length of my hardening cock. "Turn on the dildo, I made sure it was charged before delivery."

I hear the vibration echo in her quiet room. "Put it in your mouth to wet it," I demand. She does as I say, and holy fuck! Her mouth looks perfect stretched out over the ridges that cascade down the length.

I take a deep breath trying to slow my beating heart. "Slide it inside."

"Do you want to see it?" she asks, and I am so proud of her sudden desire for exploration.

"No, baby, I want to see your face when you come all over that dick. Pretend it's mine."

I can tell when it's all the way in, because her head falls back into her pillow and her breathing quickens. She is silent, except for the small pants leaving her lips. I watch her intently as I pump up and down my length.

Her breasts move up and down with each small motion, and I can tell she is moving it around so it hits just the right spot. She moans and they get louder and louder until she screams my name and her entire body stiffens.

"Shit baby! Show me you dripping for me."

She lowers the camera so I can see her arousal glisten around the dildo, and I spill onto my stomach, goose-bumps peppering my skin.

"This," I say with a ragged breath, "this is going to be a nightly occurrence until I can have you myself."

She slides the dildo out of her and brings the screen back to her flush face. "Cash, when is that actually going to be?"

Her expression is sad and her eyes are wet with oncoming tears.

"I don't know baby, but the second I can sneak away, I'm coming for you."

I'm on probation for breaking part of my contract, but she doesn't know that yet.

My preseason and game time travel have been restrict-
ed, so I actually have no fucking idea when it will be, but
it will happen. I will make sure of it.

Even if it kills my future in baseball.

Under the Lights

"There was magic in the air, you ahd to be there"
-Megan Moroney and Kenny Chesney

April

"WHAT TIME DOES YOUR flight land? I want to pick you up at the airport if I can," Cash's voice is velvety and smooth as he talks to me on FaceTime while I pack my bags.

"I land at 11:15. You'll still be at the field," the words escape my mouth in a sigh that I didn't intend for him to hear.

We have been dating for several months, and it's opening weekend. I don't want my internal disappointment of not seeing him the second I land to put a damper on his moment.

"Tulip, I will meet you at my apartment the second I get done with practice," he reassures me.

"I can't wait to see you," I offer him a smile. Because it's true. I can't wait to see him. Between my bakery and his schedule, building a long distant relationship and not really having any time together since the wedding is hard. He came back a month ago, but shit, it was just for two days, and we spent the entire time in my bed.

"Are you sure you're ok closing the bakery for the weekend?" Concern for my business fills his voice.

"Cash, I'm a planner. Trust me, I am so excited to see you play, I have been saving extra money to make sure I won't miss a beat. Plus, I made some extra pastries for L&L. Blake's got plenty to sell for me through the weekend."

"I just want to make sure you are taken care of." He smiles, and I can't wait to see it in person. I miss it.

"What's the first thing on the docket?" I ask, eager to hear about all the fancy baseball things we will get to do this weekend.

"We are meeting my parents for dinner after my practice. Then I'm taking you home." He leaves the insinuation lingering in the air, and my body reacts in the most delicious way.

"Well in that case, I better shower before I head to the airport," I suggest as I finish putting my last few items in my suitcase.

"What's the point? I'm just going to make you join me for one when I get home from practice." I hear the desire bubbling to the surface as he speaks.

"Way to twist my arm. I guess I'll have to use the extra time to grab a coffee," I tease.

"Absolutely. Get good and caffeinated for me, babe. We have a long night ahead of us."

"The fuck you are." I hear Cash's echo across the apartment as I let myself in, and panic sets in. What is going on?

I throw bags down in the doorway and rush towards the direction of his voice.

He's in his bedroom, pacing back and forth as his phone sits on speaker on the dresser. His hair is a mess, I can tell he's been running his hands through it.

He turns towards me as the voice on the other end picks up so quickly it interrupts his attempt to place a kiss to my lips.

"I don't know who the fuck you think you are, Cash, but there are a shit ton of talented ball players foaming at the mouth waiting to be a part of this team. If I say we're sending another player to be the face of the foundation, that's what is happening."

I don't know who he's talking to, but they are obviously pissed.

"A minor league player is not going to have the same draw as me. At least send another player on the team."

"The minors have more flexibility. I was telling you as a courtesy, not obligation. Get iced up, rest, and be ready to go tomorrow."

The man hangs up, and Cash throws his phone on the bed.

"I'm sorry," I say, placing a kiss on his cheek.

"It's not your fault." His eyes are red and he looks tired.

"If I didn't make you go to Jamaica, you'd still have the foundation. It's a little my fault."

He pulls me into a hug, "If you didn't ask me to go to Jamaica, I wouldn't have you, and that would be so much worse."

"True." I laugh, trying to change the mood. "I was expecting you to meet me here much later. I thought practice would last longer the day before a game."

"Yeah, Coach took it a little easy today so we could be fresh for tomorrow."

"Where are we meeting your parents?" I ask, a little nervous. I've never met someone's parents before.

"We're getting hotdogs around the corner from the stadium. It's tradition."

"I love traditions."

"Me too." He smiles and it looks a little brighter than a few minutes ago.

"Let's make one for ourselves," I suggest grabbing him by the hand and leading him out of the room. "I figured we'd be doing a lot of traveling back and forth, so I got you something."

I open my carry on and pull out a bag of seeds. "I stopped to buy some snacks for the plane, and I figured you could take them to the game with you tomorrow."

"You got snacks." His smile is even bigger this time.

"Let's surprise each other with some snacks each time one of us travels to see each other."

"I love that. What did you get yourself?" he asks.

"Well someone turned me on to blueberry muffin protein bars," I say, pulling out the box.

"You didn't eat them this time either," he laughs.

"Yeah, I'm a nervous traveler."

"You want our tradition to be snacks that you don't eat?"

"Yeah, it's cute, remember?"

Cash

"This is my new favorite smell," I whisper, as I run the fluffy sponge thingy with body wash over her skin. "Brown sugar."

"You soaping me up is pretty amazing." Her voice is slow and relaxed.

I have learned that patience and anticipation is the best way to ensure she has an enjoyable experience every time we are intimate. While I want nothing more than to press her against this wall and sink inside her, I know that will only be for my benefit. So instead I slow my pace and run featherlike touches up and down her skin.

I watch the water run in rivulets down her back and the sight is captivating. The way the water runs quickly before disappearing into her skin.

"What is this called?" I ask running the sponge over her nipples, circling them a few times.

"It's a luffa." She lets out a small giggle.

"Luffa," I repeat slowly as I move it down her stomach, just above my favorite spot. Pausing just before I sweep it over her hip and across her lower back, I watch as her skin becomes sprinkled with tiny little goose bumps.

"Cash," she whispers my name, and the sound tests my resolve.

"Hmmm?"

"Why are you teasing me?"

"Not teasing, baby. Just making sure you feel good."

"I would feel better if you threw that damn luffa down and replaced it with your hands."

"We have to shower so we can go meet my parents, Tulip."

"Do you really want me all keyed up when I meet your mom?" She places her hand on my chest and turns little circles with the tip of her finger.

"I want you keyed up when I bring you home." I kiss her on the nose and finish washing the soap off her body.

"You are such a tease." She laughs. I'm such a sucker for her laugh.

"Do you like hotdogs?" my dad asks April as we find a seat in the small restaurant. The tables are covered in sticky plastic, and the chairs are ripped.

I love Micky's so much, but seeing it through fresh eyes makes me a little uneasy. What if she hates it? What if she misses the charm, the baseball cards covering the walls, the old stadium chairs that sit around each table?

"Hot dogs are one of my dad's favorite foods. We grill them all the time back home, they remind me of home. My favorite is to top them with grilled onions and peppers."

"You'll have to get it San Diego style," Mom adds. "They wrap it in bacon on a toasted bun and smother it in onions and peppers."

"That sounds like a dream." April closes her eyes and smiles. "Everything is better with bacon.

Those words leave her mouth, and I think I'm in love.

I can't see her from the field, but knowing that she is here as I step up to the plate for the first time this season makes my heart skip.

I step into the box and take my stance. It's a routine, habit, but today it feels different. There is just something special about having someone special rooting for you, waiting for you. It gives each motion a different purpose.

"Ball!" the ump yells.

I readjust my stance and look the pitcher right in the eye. I can tell by the way he adjusts his grip that this one is coming hard across the plate.

I step and swing, and the crack of the bat fills the space around me. It's one of the best sounds in the entire world. Crips and clean.

The ball slides across the dirt and I only look at it for a second before I am certain it's sliding right past short to the grass. I take off running and when my cleats cross first base I hear my second favorite sound on the field. A rubbery crack as the bottom of my cleats make a muffled slide across the bag.

I look up into the box I know my parents and April are in, and instantly see her jumping up and down, her smile as bright as the sun just before it disappears behind my mom when she pulls April into a giant hug.

My heart skips a beat. That's my new favorite view from the field.

Falling Apart or Coming Together?

One and half years later

"This is our house, we make the rules"

-Taylor Swift

April

"April, when was the last time you were sexually active?" Dr. Anderson asks.

"About a month ago. Cash went back to San Diego for spring training, why?"

It's been two months since I had my period, and this is the longest I have gone without one. The timing isn't always exactly the same, but it comes, so I made an appointment.

In the tiny dark corner of my mind, the only place I allow myself to hold it, I am curious if I could be pregnant.

Deciding to lean into the heavy stuff instead of pushing it away, I speak up, "Is there a chance I could be pregnant?"

"Yes, but," she says, rolling on her stool from where she was typing on her computer, so she is right in front of me. She places her hand on mine to comfort me, and my stomach drops. I know she means to be a source of strength, I have been her patient for almost 5 years. She knows me well, but right now, her motions and words are causing my body to tense. "You are on hormones, and if you are pregnant, you would need to stop taking them. The risks for things like blood clots and abnormal placenta development are too high. Over time it could cause fetal development to be impacted, and you'd likely miscarry."

"*Yes,*" her initial word rings through my head.

I thought if I ever heard it, I would be on top of the world. But right now, I don't know what emotion I'm holding.

My heart is pounding. My hands are clammy. I don't understand, she said I could get pregnant, there was a small chance. I feel a small bead of sweat trickle down my temple, and just at that moment my phone pings and I see a preview of a text from Cash on my screen. He doesn't know I'm here.

Cash: I love you.

He sends me a good morning text every morning, but today it came at the exact time I needed it.

I look up from my phone and gather my thoughts before I speak. "I don't understand, you said there was a chance I could still get pregnant."

"April, this is why I keep asking you what support system you have at home. Recommending someone to come with you to your appointments. It's hard for patients themselves to hear all of the information and take it in." She moves back over to her computer and starts typing something. She is quiet for a few moments before she moves back. "I will print some literature about pregnancy while on hormone replacement therapy, that you can take a read. I suggest you and Cash go over it together. But, April, I need you to hear me. There is a chance you could be pregnant, but if you are, your body will not be able to sustain the pregnancy. You would likely miscarry," her voice is kind but firm. "I will have your results in a few minutes, but I'll go grab that information while we wait."

The door clicks behind her, and the finality of that comes with it, steals my breath. Part of me always held on to this false little sliver of hope.

A few minutes later she comes back in with the papers, and sits down in front of me.

"You are not pregnant." She pauses so I can catch up to her words. "The pregnancy blood test came back negative. Your labs indicate decreased function of your ovaries. However, your hormone levels are consistent. The hormones will not slow the progression, they are there to mitigate the symptoms. This is just a part of this condition. As your ovaries continue to lose function, your periods will get farther apart."

I look at her, but I don't say anything. I just shake my head and stand up, taking the papers she left me.

"April," she calls after me as I open the door.

When I turn to look at her she asks, "Do you want me to call you a ride?"

"No, I'll be fine." I reassure her as I walk out.

I pull out my phone and reply to Cash.

April: I love you. Call me after your game.

Blake and Ana texted to see if I wanted to go to the zoo with them today.

Blake and Luke had Maverick a few months ago. Is he even old enough to go to the zoo?

I shake my head. This has become my life. Going on baby dates with my two best friends and their kids. Only right now, I don't want to be the extra wheel on a baby train I may never actually get to board. So, I declined. Said I had to work. Which I should do. I hired a small staff so I could travel to Cash's games and they are great. It practically runs itself, but maybe going in and baking this morning will get my mind off things.

When I get to the bakery and put flour on the counter, the cloud of dust provides a blanket of clarity.

I need to be doing more of what I love. I'm fucking chasing a man across the country so he can live his dream, watching my friends and family build lives, and I'm just letting it all slip passed me. For what?

I spend the next few hours filling the room with croissants. They're not fancy, but they are one of my favorite comfort foods. I make a few dozen, place some in the rack, and some in the freezer, talk a little with the girls working today, and then head home.

It's on my way home, I realize, this feeling that I have stirring around me is loneliness. I'm just going through the motions.

Existing, but not living.

I open my phone and send another text to Cash, knowing he won't get it until after his game.

April: Today was a terrible day. I needed you, and you are so far away. I'm just existing here. I want to build a life, Cash. Not just exist.

I close my phone and walk to my car.

Cash

"WHO THE FUCK SENDS a text like that and then doesn't answer the mother fucking phone?" I curse as I redial her number for the hundredth time.

I got done with the game, got showered, and when I got back to the locker room to call her, that fucking text from hours ago was on the screen.

The months I'm off season are great. I go back to Vermont. I'm closer to my parents, I stay with April. But fuck, during the season it's hard.

I'm losing her.

"The fuck I am," I push the thought away, and drive to my place to pack a bag. We have a few days free. I'll go back and be with her for a few days. See what's going on.

When I get home, I rush inside ready to throw anything I have clean into a bag, when I realize that the scent of brown sugar permeates the room. The smell is undeniable, it lingers in the air, a comfort I miss when we're apart.

"April?!" I yell as I look around the living room and kitchen looking for any concrete evidence that she is here. But I come up empty. There is not one single thing out of place, I look over to the corner where she always places her shoes, I search for her keys on the rack. Nothing.

I'm imagining it. I'm such a fucking mess right now, that I am imagining things.

I grab my suitcase out of the closet and go to the bathroom to pack my toothpaste and deodorant.

"I'll just grab a few things. I can do laundry there," I tell myself as I walk into my room.

"Where are you off to?" she asks with a smile. "I just got here."

I take a deep breath and take her in. She's laying in my bed in a pair of sleep shorts and one of my t-shirts, scrolling on her phone.

"Oh, thank fuck," I let out. "What the hell was that text? Why were you ignoring my calls?" My tone is full of irritation, and she knows it.

"I'm sorry. In my head, this was romantic. I wanted to surprise you." She leans in to kiss me, but I pull away.

"What is going on?" I notice the bag of seeds laying next to her on the bed and a single blueberry muffin protein bar. This time it's half eaten.

"You are such a pain in the ass sometimes, do you know that?" I say to her, because she is being way too nonchalant right now.

But, fuck do I love her.

"Cash, I avoid things, because I don't know what to say."

"I know," I say, acknowledging the obvious.

"I don't want to do that anymore. I don't want to live in this constant state of being in my own damn way. So," she takes a breath. "I'm going to tell you everything on my mind."

I sit down and focus, knowing whatever is about to leave her mouth will do so at a million miles a minute and I need to focus.

She begins, and sure as shit, her words appear to be firing out of a cannon. "I haven't had a period in two months. I went to the doctor, and she said I'm not pregnant. That I can get pregnant, but I'll most likely lose it. This is apparently just a part of it, my life." She wipes a tear.

"Anyways, I was devastated, and all I wanted was you, but you are so fucking far away. Then I turned down a zoo date with the girls because I can't be a mom too, and I went to the bakery, and I realized I'm following you around while you chase your dreams, but I haven't been at the bakery consistently in a while to chase mine." Her voice is wobbly, and her hands are shaking.

She's breaking up with me.

I reach out for her hand, and she moves in a little closer, making me feel a little more easy.

"I won't be that girl, Cash. I'm done just existing because it's too hard to say the hard stuff. I need to be with someone and still be all the things I want to be. I can't keep leaving my dreams behind for yours."

There it is.

"April—" I say, but she shushes me with her finger.

"Cash, I decided that both of our dreams are too important to miss."

"No, we can figure something out, Tulip." Tears start to prick my eyes.

"Cash, I want to open a second location for The Daily Bite. Here. Can I move in with you?"

I blink a few times trying to catch up. "For real?" I ask. "Are you fucking with me?" She tends to do that when shit gets heavy.

She laughs and it fills the room. "No, I'm not fucking with you. Everyone is building a life, and I want to too. Cash, I wander around Vermont like a lonely shell of myself. My life is here, watching you play, eating hotdogs, and expanding my business."

"What if we do even better than that?" I ask. Kissing her.

"I'm always up for something even better." She smiles.

I stand up and walk over to my closet.

"Are you already clearing out space for me?" she asks with a laugh. "I didn't bring a bag. I only have the few things I left here."

I walk out with a ring tied to a piece of paper I've had for a few weeks. I didn't know how we were going to make it work. But I knew I wanted to.

The ring is simple, a silver band with one square diamond. Classic and timeless.

"Be my wife. Tulip."

I hand her the ring and paper, and her eyes well up with tears. "You have it all filled out? This is what you want?"

"This is exactly what I want."

A few months ago when Maverick was born, there was a baby at the hospital being adopted. April's eyes lit up. *"I want to do that one day, give a baby a home,"* she whispered.

When I got home, I printed out the application for adoption through the state for both California and Vermont. I figured once I proposed, we could decide where we wanted to make a home, and turn it in.

"We just have to sign it. It's a lengthy process, but we can take it in on Monday. I want to make a family with you, Tulip."

She smiles, and moves in close to me, until her voice is just a whisper away. "Don't you see, babe, I came here because I want to make a life with you too. Of course I'll be your wife, and Cash—" she smiles, "I get to be a mom."

She does a little happy dance, and I laugh.

When her mom asked her why she didn't want to go through a private agency some day, her answer was clear…

"Everyone wants a newborn baby. I want a family, and there are so many little kids just waiting for one of their own. If I get to build mine, I want to change a life."

If I *get* to…

There she was, my Tulip, finally opening up, and not just to me.

Epilogue –

Three Years Later

"I'll never beat the view, of my front porch lookin' in"

-Lonestar

Cash

"LISTEN, I GOTTA GO," I tell Knox as I pull up to my house. "I just got home, and by the looks of it, there is a lot of maintenance that needs to be done after two weeks away."

We are in the playoffs for the world series, and won the 7 game series 4-3. Which means I will be back on the road in a few days.

"I'm not gonna lie, I'm glad I missed all that shit, not being able to go pro!" Knox laughs.

"Lucky bastard." I joke. "Talk to you later."

"Enjoy your time home," he says before he hangs up.

I take in my new house, built a little over a year ago, and it's looking rough. The grass is yellowing, the weeds are overgrown and there is a dead flower pot hanging from the porch. "Fuck, I need to do something with that," I sigh.

I'm instantly overwhelmed by the amount of shit I need to do while I'm home for a few days. Maybe, Knox is right, and I need to hire someone to take care of the lawn and shit while I'm gone.

I reach up and pull the pot off the hook and set it on the ground next to the stairs so I will remember to put it in the trash on trash day.

When I stand up, my world spins, and all of the worry and stress, and the list of things I have to do melts away like dirt in the rain.

She doesn't see me. She's too focused on the chaos in front of her. April is sitting at the kitchen table, hair in a messy little knot on top of her head, a stained Sun Cats shirt, and little sleep shorts I can barely see, but want to peel off her. Lily is on her hip, and Lucy is smearing applesauce all over her highchair tray. I'm guessing applesauce is what is covering my love.

I lean against the porch rail, cross my arms and watch.

She's talking to them both softly, patiently, with a spoon in one hand, baby in the other, like she was made for this type of multitasking. As Lucy grabs the spoon from April's grip and throws it on the floor, her new favorite game, April doesn't even flinch. She just sighs and tucks a loose strand of bright blond hair behind her ear and kisses them both on the top of the head after she fastens Lily into her chair.

As she walks over to the sink, there is something about the way she moves that makes me stir inside. I have been gone far too long.

The picture on the wall right across from the door is in perfect view, and it makes me smile. It's the day the girl's adoption was finalized, just before the season started. It's been hard to find a balance, but it's worth every second.

It takes me back to the first day we laid eyes on them, a little over a year ago.

"Cash, Cash!" April's voice was a shriek, and I came running into the living room and instantly cataloged the tears flowing down her face. "They called. They're on their way. Twin girls."

"Holy shit! Just now? Out of nowhere?" I started frantically washing the dishes in the sink.

"What are you doing?" She laughed.

"We can't have dishes in the sink, Tulip."

"Cash, look at me. I don't give a shit about the dishes in the sink. Just throw them away, we only have one carseat and crib."

"Shit." We'd been waiting for this call for almost a year, and said we'd take siblings, but logistically only planned on one baby.

"We have one hour. We need to run to the store to get baby food, diapers, and another fucking stroller, highchair, and all the other shit we need." Her voice changed to panic.

"Baby food?" I asked, confused.

"Cash, you always focus on the most miniscule detail."

"How old are they?"

"Seven months."

"I don't know anything about babies. I only read about newborns." My voice was full of panic.

"Ok. Cash, focus, We cannot both freak out. One of us has to be the calm one, the voice of reason, and we both know that's not me."

I took a long breath and closed my eyes. "Right," I whispered to myself.

I turned to her and recounted all the things they told us at our last home visit. "They said they would bring us all the essentials, so all we need to get tonight is another car seat and crib. We can go to the store tomorrow."

"We can't go to the store tomorrow, they'll be here." Her voice was so loud it hurt my ears.

"Baby. We will have to go to the store and work, and all the things with babies. We can't just stay home."

"We need a sitter!" she cried. "We don't have a sitter."

I bent down and placed my hands on both sides of her face. "We planned for this, remember? We both are taking a few weeks leave."

"Right." She took a few long breaths.

After she calmed down, we went to the store and got all the things we needed, and a few things we didn't, and when we pulled back into the driveway, our entire world changed.

Time stood still. 3:23 pm.

That was the moment I became a dad. Not in a conventional way in a hospital room filled with doctors and nurses, but right there in my front yard, holding hands with my wife, staring at two sets of identical blue eyes surrounded by little freckles. One with blond curly hair and the other with dark brown waves. Two mirror images of April and I, like all the stars aligned—they were our baby girls.

I hear Lily laugh, and it sounds so much like April's it pulls me from my thoughts.

I peel myself away from my view so I can be part of the beautiful mess inside.

"It smells like applesauce in here." Lucy's laugh bubbles out when she sees me, and I swear, I could quit baseball tomorrow if it meant I got to hear that every day.

I pick her up and laugh as I give Lily big kisses before heading over to my Tulip.

"Yeah, well I hope you like it. I think it's in my hair," April's tone is playful and warm. I get closer and also smell the faint smell of cinnamon.

"You're sexy, especially when you have sticky shit in your hair," I tease. "You also smell like cinnamon rolls."

"Don't be a horn dog in front of the girls, the smell is a perk from being a mom and owning the hottest bakery in San Diego." She laughs, and I love when she's a little cocky.

"They should know how lucky they are to have a hot mom."

"I'm pretty sure my level of hotness has no impact on them whatsoever."

"Hell yeah it does. It makes their dad happy, and as they get older, the more preoccupied I am with you, the more shit they'll get away with."

"They might be more excited that they have a hot-shot professional baseball player for a dad," she jokes.

"I know *you* get excited by that," I say, wiggling my brows.

She shoves me playfully and walks over to wipe down the table.

"You know, one perk of my job is a team nanny," I say, pulling the rag out of her hand and wiping up the mess. "Let's have her watch the girls tomorrow night so I can have you to myself for a bit," I suggest as I lean in and give her a kiss. "Go get in the shower. It's late, and you need a minute to yourself. Plus, I want to make sure you are nice and clean before I dirty you up. I'll put the girls to bed."

She doesn't protest the time alone to take a hot shower without crying babies. She hurries towards the stairs, and I call after her when my phone pings with a notification.

"Tulip." She turns on her heels and looks at me. "There is a package on the porch. It was just delivered."

She tilts her head and offers me a crooked smile before opening the door.

"Don't you dare open that until the girls are in bed. I have all kinds of delicious plans for you tonight."

She winks and sets the box on the table in the entryway. Then she turns and walks up the stairs with a little sway to her hips, just enough to let me know this night won't end quietly.

I watch her go, a familiar warmth settling in my chest, the kind that grows in the quiet moments.

Outside, the porch creaks faintly in the wind. The package waits, silent and unassuming. I reach for it, but don't open it. Not yet. Instead, I turn off the light, take a deep breath, and smile.

Some things—like the contents of that box, can wait.

But her?

Never.

I clean the girls up and rock them both to sleep in record time, so April can unwrap her gift.

After all this time there is one thing I am certain of, we may have started under a veil of secrets. But it was just the beginning. Proof that even the smallest spark can light the way to something extraordinary.

Acknowledgments

First and foremost, thank you—yes, *you*, the reader. Your time is valuable, and the fact that you've chosen to spend some of it with this book means the world to me. Your support, curiosity, and imagination are what breathe life into these pages. I don't take that lightly. Thank you, from the bottom of my heart.

To my family, your love, encouragement, and patience have been the quiet engine behind this journey. Thank you for standing by me during the late nights, the rewrites, and the occasional doubts. Your belief in me never wavered, even when mine did.

To my beta readers, Heather Newsome, Evelyn Charles, Lindsey Kelley, Melanie McNair, Kristina Jarman, Chrissie Goss, and Alyssa Trujillo, you are the unsung heroes. Thank you for your sharp eyes, honest feedback, and for catching what I couldn't. You challenged me to go deeper and pushed this story to be better. Your insight helped shape the heart of this book.

To my editor, JJ, thank you for bringing clarity to chaos. Your guidance, precision, and care have elevated this story more than words can say. You didn't just polish the book, you helped me become a better writer.

I also want to extend a very special thank you to Lindsey R. Without you, Cash would not be the man he is. You set him in motion, and helped me develop a man for the ages.

To everyone who worked tirelessly along the way, this book is as much yours as it is mine.

With deepest gratitude and love,
Harper Rae